THE NICHE
Twin Flame Mysteries

Adah F. Kennon, Ph.D.

Sheba Enterprises—Las Vegas, NV
ISBN: 978-0-578-81391-2
Library of Congress Control Number: 2020923715
Title: The Niche, Twin Flame Mysteries
Author: Adah F. Kennon, Ph.D.
Digital distribution | 2020
Paperback | 2020

This is a work of fiction. The characters, names, incidents, places, and dialogue are products of the author's imagination, and are not to be construed as real.

Dedication

Dedicated with love to my twin flame, W.B.H. and
my spirit guides … you know who you are….

Chapter 1

"I didn't do anything," Sheila moaned. She'd been in the room for less than one hour and the atmosphere was already making her uncomfortable. The long conference table in front of her was the only place she could rest her arms, and it was no secret that what looked-like a wall mirror was actually glass on one side, hiding a space where people sat in the darkness and watched her with suspicious eyes. She reached for the box of tissue on the table, pulled-out a few, and played with them until they almost disintegrated in her sweating hands.

Detective Patterson did a lot of overtime that week and the stress was beginning to show. His chair had a cushion, but his lumbago was flaring-up and he was already uncomfortable. He wondered how much more he could endure before his body failed. Dressed as he was in long pants, a long-sleeved white dress shirt, black tie and blazer, he longed for the time to pass so he could go home, put some heat on his back and take a muscle relaxant. Short on patience, he wasn't too sympathetic to Sheila's plight as he watched her shifting nervously in the folding chair, trying in vain to get into a comfortable position. *She acts like she doesn't have a clue why she's being detained.* As the prime suspect in a murder case, the idea was that she be made as uncomfortable as possible.

His instincts told him that this was certainly not going to be an average run-of-the-mill investigation. Once the interview was completed, all that remained was for the forensic unit to finish their sweep of the crime scene, including evidence that her fingerprints were all over that gun. That would be all he needed to form probable cause, take her into custody and book her. Until then, he was stuck at the station. But, on the other hand, the picture wasn't entirely bleak. His winning track record was the highest in the department. Another victory would insure his chance of making sergeant and he could definitely use the raise. He would be stoic and bear his discomfort in silence.

"Do you understand your rights, Mrs. Palmer?"

"Yes, I want to cooperate."

"Good, that's commendable." Not wanting to do anything that would get the case thrown out of court on a technicality, he added, "Would you like to have an attorney present? If you don't have one, we can arrange for someone to come in."

"No, I'm ok for now. I just want to talk, get it all off my chest. I don't have anything to hide."

"Very well," he said. "I need to get a statement from you." Reaching for a pen and one of the note pads on the table, Detective Patterson reviewed the facts out-loud as he wrote. "We got a call from the caretaker at the cemetery about … three hours ago. And what did we find when we got there? Let's review the laundry list - two dead bodies on the floor next to an unlicensed Glock 22 handgun, recently fired; one man, still alive but oozing blood and in serious condition; shattered glass, pieces of some kind of jar and ... uh, what looked like *ashes* all over the floor; and you, running around, hysterical, looking like the cat who ate the canary. Oh, and let's not forget a glass wall with a great big hole in it. We're not sure what caused it ... maybe it was gun fire but maybe ... something else ... like what caused it broke-out from *behind* the glass?" Laughing nervously, he added, "Of course, that's impossible, right?"

"Uh, that space behind the glass - it's called a niche. That broken jar was the cremation urn stored in that niche. And, those really were ashes on the floor."

"Sorry," he muttered, clearly annoyed at being corrected. "Did I leave anything out, Mrs. Palmer?"

"No, but that's just the beginning. There's a lot more that I need to tell you."

"Don't worry, you'll have an opportunity to tell your story. I like to summarize things every so often, just so everyone is on the same page. What I read is what we have so far." Handing the note pad to her, he said, "Please look this over and sign on the line if you agree. My cursive isn't so hot, so I printed everything. Let me know if you need me to go over any of it for you."

Sheila gave the page a quick once-over. "That looks ok. Sign here?" she said, pointing to the line he had drawn close to bottom of the page.

"Uh, yes, right there." Making sure that her signature was legible, Detective Patterson carefully tore that sheet from the pad, placed it in one of the pockets of the expanding file on the table and secured everything with a long rubber band. Going through the formalities gave him plenty of time to gather his thoughts. His blue eyes fixed on Sheila, he said, "I'll be honest with you. I don't know how to make heads or tails of this case. Look, let's cut to the chase. I think we can both agree that there has been a crime. What *really* happened in there? Oh, I forgot to tell you, I'm turning the tape-recorder on. It's routine." He pushed one of the buttons, settled back in his chair and said, "Whenever you're ready."

"Where should I start?" asked Sheila.

Looking at the wall clock directly behind her, the hint of a smile creased the corners of his mouth. "How about, at the beginning."

"Well, there was a dream I kept having ..."

"What?"

"A dream. You said that I should start at the beginning."

Detective Patterson was anxious to get home. His wife was holding dinner for him and he wanted to see his kids. But, it was obvious that he was in for another long evening. Gritting his teeth, he steeled himself. "Yes, so I did. Go ahead, Mrs. Palmer."

"Well, I don't know why but I kept having the same damn dream. I'm driving to a cemetery in terrible weather - maybe rainy? The trip is uneventful. I drive for about five miles through city traffic, then make the first left turn onto a gravel road that passes between tall brass gates guarded on either side by well-aged angelic-like figures, spattered with years of bird poop. I sense that another world lies beyond those gates inviting me to enter and leave my troubles behind, at least for a while. I continue and soon come to a small lot next to two buildings. One seems to be a small house of some kind. The other is a one-story

4

building that looks like a chapel. I pull into the first available space. The front door of the chapel is dwarfed by a tall flag-pole which proudly sports a slightly tattered American flag. I park, roll-down my window and sit in the car taking it all in. Time passes. It all feels so ... melancholy. I hear the sound of a long chain, clanging and hollow as it hits the flagpole, the cloth billowing in a breeze that plays with it like a child would do with a toy. Trees are clustered in small groups, their leaves ranging in colors from pale lime to emerald green. More time passes. Eventually I leave my car and walk down a stone-paved path winding its way in-between rows of headstones, some decorated with relics long-sense faded. I can just make-out the vague outline of two people, darting between the graves- maybe cleaning away debris or kneeling, lost in prayer. I can even smell the foul odor of floral arrangements lingering in the air, once alive but now in various stages of wilt and decay. Some graves are decorated with plastic flowers; but, the saddest of all are the undecorated ones, seeming to beg for someone to care for them. I want to turn back, but I feel that I must keep going. I feel that I must get to something or someone waiting for me at the end of that path. But, what it is I couldn't tell you. That's when everything fades and I wake up. Go figure."

"So ... how exactly does this dream relate to what happened tonight?" asked Detective Patterson.

"Don't you see? That dream was trying to send me a message ... that something ... weird was going to happen to me, that some... supernatural force was going to direct my actions and that I would *choose* to go along with the program. It was a... premonition. I should have paid more attention."

Detective Patterson turned off the recorder. "Just a minute, I need to stretch my leg."

Standing up and with his back turned to Sheila, he faced the one-way mirror. Pretending to check his image, he actually sent a barely visible hand signal to the person sitting on the other side. *Nutty as a fruitcake!* Then, reaching into his shirt pocket, he pulled out a crumpled package of cigarettes and a lighter. He turned back to face Sheila, his face expressionless.

"Oh, do you mind if I smoke?"

"Not at all," Sheila shrugged. It really did, but she was not about to say anything that might irritate him.

Taking one from the package, he lit it, took a long drag, exhaled the smoke and flicked a few ashes into a nearby ashtray. Returning to his chair, he pushed the record button and said, "Ok, the recorder is back on. Go ahead, I'm all ears."

"Well," said Sheila, "It all started about a year ago ..."

Chapter 2

Irritated by the smoke, Sheila took a tissue from the box on the table and wiped eyes already swollen from crying. "Excuse me, I want to cooperate. I've got nothing to hide. You look like a kind person. I've been through so much. I'm sorry, I've just got a lot on my mind."

Detective Patterson eyed Sheila as she spoke. He liked to form an initial impression of suspects, size-them-up, then look back to see how accurate it was. At this point, he would have bet his last dollar that if looking in a dictionary, her picture would be next to the word *conceited*. What she went on to say proved that would have been a sure bet.

Trying to lighten the mood, she said, "You know what they say about people with good genes - we already have what others work hard to get. Now, take me, for instance. I'm what they call a gym rat. I work-out six days each week, not because I really have to but because it keeps a sharp edge on this - *marketable product*. Just look at me," she said, "broad shoulders, slim waste, six-pack abs always showing, tight butt and sculpted calves, all wrapped-up in a five-foot nine-inch feminine frame. Shoulder-length brown curly hair, hazel eyes, and creamy tanned skin. Now, that's the kind of package any female professional body builder would kill for, don't you think?"

"Is there a point to all of this, Mrs. Palmer?"

Taking his comment as one of callous indifference, Sheila's eyes filled with tears that began to tumble down her cheeks. Seeing a woman cry always made Detective Patterson feel a bit uncomfortable. His interviewing style was legendary and often used as an example when training rookies. He knew how to control the course of the conversation - when to turn-up the heat and when to de-escalate, maybe be more compassionate and caring. Given her reaction, he softened his tone, saying, "Would you like to stop for a few minutes?"

"Just let me blow my nose…"

"Of course," he said. "Please continue when you are ready."

"Where did I stop? Oh, I remember. One morning about a year ago, I was getting ready for a major competition, and expected to win every event that I entered. I would do anything to win, no matter what it took or who it hurt. That morning, my treadmill routine was a killer. I used most of my energy to finish. I couldn't feel my legs, but I managed to slowly make my way over to one of the mirrors positioned around the main floor. I wanted to look at me. I needed to study my image. I thought to myself, *uh huh, you still got it goin on. When I step on that stage, my rhinestone-studded two-piece posing suit will leave little to the imagination. The judges will give me low marks for any fault. Deal with it now. Mirror, I hate you … but you will never lie to me. I've got to look good coming and going.* Then I saw what I needed to work on - my back. An evening session was definitely in order. But first, I needed to take a quick break to eat and rest.

I rented a small apartment, but the gym was where I spent most of my time. My place was no bigger than an up-graded storage unit. It was way below what I could afford, but close enough to the gym to justify the compromise. I could catch a few hours of sleep, take a quick shower, change clothes and eat. That day I planned to take a two-hour nap, but my body knew what it needed. I had to rush to get back to the gym when my nap turned into a six-hour marathon. With a cold, foaming protein shake in hand, I was just about to leave when my phone rang. I started to let it go to voice-mail, but something told me to see who was calling. I wasn't surprised to find that it was my training partner, Malik.

Crowing like a rooster, he said, 'Hey, Sheila baby … something has come-up. My car won't start. So, I won't be able to make it to the gym tonight.'

I didn't want him to know how annoyed I was; so, I took a deep breath before answering. 'Malik, when are you gonna buy a car you can depend on instead of that ten year-old hooptie?'

'It might be old but it still gets me where I want to go … sometimes. Anyway, I can't get there. You gonna miss me?'

Malik tried to hide his indifference, but I knew that he really didn't care one way or the other. I guess my being miserable made him feel like a big man or something, you know?"

Momentarily lost in thought, Detective Patterson said, "Yeah, I know the type."

"Well, this time I wasn't going to fall for the bait. I said, 'No, I'll survive. See you later.'

Actually, I was pissed. Malik and I grew-up in the Village, a public housing project in the Fifth Ward. Our families lived next to each other, so we spent a lot of time together during our early years, playing in the front yard and so on. It never seemed like I wanted for anything, being an only child. But Malik's parents were not that well-off and he sometimes put the beg on me for one thing or another. Our folks loved us and wanted the best for us. They tried to shield us from the ugliness in the community. The thugs were there, waiting to welcome us with open arms. They didn't have to worry about me. But, Malik was ... different. He was a really smart kid, but sometimes wrote his letters and numbers backwards. He also had some ... emotional problems."

"What kind of emotional problems?" asked Detective Patterson.

"Well, it was hard for him to keep his mind on stuff, fighting, temper tantrums, moody - things like that. It wasn't long before he lost interest in school. I was a year younger but two years ahead of him grade wise.

Malik was such a cute kid. I called him my "play" big brother but really had a puppy-dog crush on him and lived for his undivided attention. When he pouted, his hooded hazel eyes filled with tears and innocence. He could get just about anything from me that he wanted. If he didn't, he would get angry and act like he was a victim.

The years passed. Malik began spending less time with me and more time with the guys in the community, and especially his older brother, Petey. He idolized Petey and did everything he could to please him. Petey was no Einstein, but he was street smart and he loved his little brother. He was a well-known professional body builder and power-lifter, one of the best in Texas. Like most of us, he acted one way in public and another way when with his family. Strong as an ox, he worked hard and got to the point where he could easily bench-press four-hundred pounds."

"Quite an accomplishment for anyone," said Detective Patterson as he tapped his cigarette on the edge of the ashtray.

"I'll say! He virtually lived at the gym, the most popular hang-out place in our neighborhood. The guys respectfully called him, *Mr. Lucky*. Some of them swore that he strutted instead of walked, just like during competition when all eyes fell on him as the spotlight tracked his progression to center stage. That was his definition of success. A hair-trigger temper, along with a *don't mess with me* attitude, made the baddest dude in the place stop dead in his tracks, especially when he scrunched his eyes tight and pursed his lips. But at home when he let his guard down, his grin was as wide as the Gulf.

In fact, it was Petey who introduced both of us to gym life. Don't get me wrong. Working-out was my hobby, a way to keep the muscle on and fat off my body. My parents really pushed me into it. Being tops in sports was their dream for themselves. They were high school athletes but didn't have what it took to make it to the major leagues. I knew they were trying to live their dreams though me not understanding that those rewards come to only a few at the top of the food chain. But, you couldn't convince them otherwise. The plan was to treat my success as a family business. My money management skills were never great, so I'm sure they saw themselves assuming that responsibility, maybe even skimming a little off the top that I made from modeling jobs, sponsorships, and prizes. That was going to be their ticket out of the Projects. Sometimes they came to the gym to see me work-out. But, they never missed one of my competitions. That was the only time I saw their faces light-up with pride about anything I did. That was when I really felt their ... love. Anyhow, they wanted me to do it and I did as I was told. I was going to find a way to make it happen. And since I enjoyed the thrill of competition anyway, the shoe fit ... for a while.

Frankly I never really believed that was my road to success. I needed big bucks to support the kind of life I planned to live. Want to know my plan?"

Detective Patterson smiled. "Enlighten me, Mrs. Palmer."

"I set goals for myself - finish high school, then college, then land a high-paying, steady job. That's how I planned to get myself and my folks out of the Projects."

"Made sense. So how did things go?" Detective Patterson asked.

"Just as planned. I graduated from Wheatley High and then Texas Southern University. Time, effort and the right kind of educational credentials landed me my dream job as one of the highest paid fashion designers in Houston. But it was different for Malik.

My bank account was expanding and my credit score was right there at the top. Malik's rating was so bad that he couldn't get a credit card. School got harder, he lost his focus and dropped out in tenth grade. That really made it hard for him to get a good paying job the honest way.

Petey didn't take much of an interest in me, but he tried to keep close watch over Malik, determined that he would follow in his footsteps. Many of the older guys at the gym liked Malik and wanted to help with his development. They were excellent role models, men of integrity and honor. But, Petey was very … possessive. He would be the *only* one to claim bragging rights. Malik would be *his* legacy, his gift to the world when he could no longer measure up. His plan was to watch over Malik, prepare him with the only mindset worth having - one just like his, so he would be … worthy. Petey was so wrapped-up in glorifying himself that he made a big mistake. He set Malik on a pedestal and demanded that the guys give respect that was unearned. I guess that deep down inside he sensed there was something wrong with Malik but chalked-it up to immaturity. He refused to admit that his little brother had emotional problems that were getting worse as he got older. It didn't make sense, but Malik actually believed that the world owed him something that he didn't have to earn. To make things worse, he started hanging-out with the wrong crowd, mastering a whole list of bad habits. The guys saw what was happening but were afraid to say anything. Petey was so defensive and Malik was becoming more … irrational. Things went great for a while. Then, one day when Petey wasn't watching,

Malik was horsing-around with the heavy weights. He injured one of his legs so severely that it put an abrupt end to their plans.

No one came right out and said Petey's approach was partly responsible for Malik's misfortune. No one said that he failed to give Malik the guidance he needed. No one blamed him for leaving Malik alone with the heavy weights. But, Petey blamed himself for what happened. Grieving all that might have been, he soon lost his regal title to another guy waiting for a turn on the stage in the spotlight. It wasn't long after that he joined the Army and got sent overseas, somewhere around the Philippines, I think."

Chapter 3

The end of his cigarette flared red as Detective Patterson took a final drag before grounding it into the ashtray. Addicted to the habit, he reached into his pack and took-out another one which he promptly lit. Taking a long drag, he exhaled, watching the smoke as it curled above his head to finally disappear into the ceiling vent. "Now that's odd," he said. "Why would a man who was no good at taking orders join the Army?"

"Beat's me," replied Sheila. "Some of the guys at the gym even placed bets on how long it would take before he got kicked out. He didn't even last through nine weeks of Basic Training. It just wasn't in him to be a team player, especially if he had to take a backseat so others could shine. I heard that he disobeyed a direct order from his drill sergeant, got into a fight and landed in the base hospital. But, true to form, *Mr. Lucky* had his mojo working."

***

If he had to be in the hospital, then being in a single room was ideal for Petey. With his headphone on and earbuds securely in place, he could close his eyes while listening to his music, recuperating from the fight that landed him there. Then, one day, a doctor walked into his room and made him an offer that changed his life forever.

"Well, Private, my name is Dr. Edward Fernandez. I'm the cardiologist on this Ward. I've heard a lot about you." This doctor enjoyed sneaking-up on patients to see how much he could scare them. This patient was a big guy and he wanted to see him jump, maybe scream. But, he was in for a big disappointment. Petey didn't even flinch. Disappointed by his failure, Dr. Fernandez opened the file that was attached to his clipboard.

Turning-down the volume, Petey removed his ear-buds and looked at the doctor. "Oh? And what have you heard?" he asked, with a smirk on his face.

"That you are an insolent son-of-a-bitch who doesn't play well with others."

"Sounds about right," nodded Petey, wishing that he could get up and make him pay for that slight.

"Yes," replied Doctor Fernandez. He walked back to the door, closed it, then returned to the chair next to Petey's bed. Sitting down, he placed the file and clip board on the floor, crossed his legs and looked Petey dead in the eyes. "What I'm going to say to you is… confidential, just between us, understand?"

His interest aroused, Petey dropped his arrogant tone. "What do you mean?"

"I won't beat around the bush. You're in bad, bad trouble. They're getting ready to kick your butt out of here. You'll go home in disgrace, right back to where you came from, this time with a record that will put you in worse shape than you were in when you enlisted. That wouldn't be so great for your *Mr. Lucky* image now would it? But …"

Petey glared at him with a frown and said, "Slow down, man. What did you just call me?"

The insinuation hit home. Dr. Fernandez smiled, "Never mind. I'm going to make you an offer. You've got street smarts and muscles. I like that. I can use a man like you in my ... business."

"What ... business?"

"Well, let's just say that I have certain ... tastes that call for more money than my Army pay. Get my drift? There's something about you that makes me think we have that in common. Am I right?"

"Go on, I'm listening."

"We... uh, I *acquire* swell cars over here and send them back on transport planes for sale. I set-up the deals on this side and I have a partner who represents me in Houston, you know, goes to auctions where the sales take place. We stash the profits in off-shore accounts. There's no way to trace them."

"Oh," said Petey. "So what do you need me for?"

"I need someone to actually move the merchandise from one place to another while it's still here, maybe hide stuff in out-of-the-way places until the transport date, you dig?"

"Yeah, I dig. So what will you do for me?" asked Petey.

"Don't worry, you'll get a good share of the profits and I can also get you something other than a dishonorable discharge. I have *friends* in high places. Besides, wouldn't your younger brother ... uh, Malik, is it?... love to see you successful? Interested?"

Petey's eyes grew large. "How do you know about Malik?" he snapped.

"Never you mind. How about it?"

Petey weighed his options. That doctor was right. He enlisted to improve his chances in life, not minimize them. "Count me in. Bye the way, who's this other guy?"

"Thomas Palmer. That's all you need to know for now."

Chapter 4

Trying his best to come up with a question that fit, Detective Patterson asked, "How did Malik take what happened at the gym and his brother leaving to join the Army?"

"Are you kidding?" replied Sheila. "Malik's world was in ruins. Anxious as he was to win his brothers approval, how was he going to please him now? What could he do to get back into his good graces? All options considered, there could be only one answer. It was ambitious but worth a try. He turned his attention to me. We sometimes ran into each other at the gym. After exchanging greetings, we would go our separate ways. This went on for years. I had no idea that he secretly watched my development, apparently with considerable interest.

Everything he did was self-serving. He knew that I had potential and probably figured that he had some magical powers of persuasion or something. The catch was that he needed to convince me that he was my savior, that I would only make it to the top if I let him help me. I would do all of the work and he would take the credit for my success. Petey was overseas, but that didn't matter. The news would get to him. Weeks passed, with Malik never doubting that this would allow his big brother to save face, perhaps brag that his hard work had not been entirely waisted. That would be his road to redemption.

That kind of logic appealed to Malik. He didn't need to admit his own weaknesses or accept responsibility for the mistakes he had made. All that he had to do was keep me mesmerized, make me his doormat and walk all over me. My feelings were of no consequence - it was his world. That was *his* game plan.

One day Malik cornered me at the gym and asked me if he could be my training partner. He said that he could help me get ready for my competition."

Drumming his pen on the table, Detective Patterson asked, "Didn't you think that things might be different now that you were both adults?"

"I'm not a fool," scoffed Sheila. "I know that people often change as they get older. When it came to Malik, I was stuck in the past. When I looked at him, I saw the cute little boy with those hooded hazel eyes who was my childhood friend, nothing more. Actually I probably cared more about him than he ever cared about me. But, I soon found out that he not only wanted to use me but also had romantic feelings for me which were definitely one-sided.

I asked him how his leg was and if he really felt up to it. He practically begged me to just give him a chance. But, the way he said it should have warned me that he had a hidden agenda."

"What do you mean?" asked Detective Patterson.

"Well, he mumbled. That wasn't like him. And, his eyes … he looked at me in a way that made me think that my eyes were playing tricks on me. There was no innocence, only a seductive invitation. There was something else that, for a moment sent a cold shiver down my spine. What I saw reminded me of the cunning stare of the rats we hated in the Projects. It was so pronounced and so unsettling that I had to turn away. I wondered who this man was.

I needed time to compose myself. Thankfully a woman was training next to me. I turned to watch her, pretending to be interested in her technique. When I turned back, Malik's eyes had regained their usual non-threatening hooded appearance. Against my better judgement, I consented. I wanted to give him a chance. I tried to convince myself that he wanted to do right by me. After all, it was just going to be a professional relationship. What harm could it do? I never figured he would use me to accomplish his goals. I didn't want to believe that he could be so ... cold.

Malik couldn't wait to get started. Destined to walk different paths in life, the distance between us had grown wider with each year. A lot of catching-up had to be done. So, the first thing he did was arrange his work-out schedule to accommodate my regular hours at the gym. It didn't take long for him to discover that my ego had become, shall we say, over-inflated."

Detective Patterson smiled and jokingly said, "Now who could possibly imagine that happening to a body-builder?"

Doing her best to appear wounded, Sheila said, "Personally I didn't see any cause for alarm. Things were going well because I knew what to do and how to do it. Case closed."

Sheila could see the twinkle in his blue eyes through the small puffs of smoke drifting across the table. "Oh excuse me, your royal highness," he said. "Please continue."

"Malik was not going to let anything slip under his radar. He became my shadow. He followed me everywhere, looking for any opportunity to burst my bubble and then build it up again, *Malik style*. Unfortunately, *Malik style* meant plenty of criticism and public humiliation. Being cruel and wanting to see me grovel was just his way. I blocked-out as much as possible. Now I realize that the reason I stayed around him was because I was trying to hold onto those childhood memories. I guess Petey and I had that in common.

Time went on and Malik's ways began to get on my nerves. I started calling him the *obnoxious* one, just to see if I could rattle him without causing a scene. His favorite saying was, 'Sure you need to increase the weight each time you work-out to develop muscle. But, you're doing it the wrong way. Do what I say and you'll always stay on top. Protect your guns while you grow them. Trust me, otherwise you might hurt yourself and you won't like the pain. Don't knock yourself out of the competition before you even walk onto the stage.' "

Chapter 5

Sheila continued talking about Malik, her long face showing the extent of her disappointment with the training deal.

"Many of my competitors trained at the same gym where I worked-out. Competitors could be worse than a pack of hungry wolves, constantly evaluating each other's strengths and weaknesses to beef-up their own training programs. I wanted Malik to help me walk a tight rope, nurture my self-esteem while hiding my development from prying eyes. But, he didn't know how to ... nurture. It wasn't long before the cat got out of the bag. The way that I carried myself was a dead giveaway. I never settled for being second best. I couldn't help it. Malik wouldn't let me, except when comparing myself with him. He insisted that I give him his propers. I could have whatever was left-over.

I'll have to give him credit. With his help, I increased the gains I was already making. Malik provided that extra push I needed to complete movements with the heavier weights. But, that particular night his absence meant that I would have no back-up. I had to use my head or his prediction might come true. That would definitely get back to him and he would make my life a living hell. But, what the heck, I really wasn't afraid of the physical pain. I just didn't want to be ... humiliated ... fail, not be able to finish what I started. When I left my apartment, I told myself that, if necessary, someone would come to my rescue."

"So what happened when you got to the gym?" asked Detective Patterson.

"The evening session was in full swing when I walked onto the main floor. Men and women of all shapes and sizes crowded together, straining and contorting their bodies as they jockeyed for a few feet of personal space. I could hear the faint hum of the air conditioner struggling to disperse the scent of rancid sweat that pierced the air. I pushed my way through the crowd, looking for a bench that was unoccupied. Just as I was about to lose hope, I saw one that was free and so close to the air conditioner that I could feel the breeze on my face.

I turned around and heard someone yell 'Look-out, *Miss Thing* is in the house!' I knew that it had to be one of the guys huddled around the weight rack. Understand that my goal was to be at the top of the heap. I wasn't after their friendship, I was after their respect, not as a courtesy but in recognition of what I had done to earn it. They saw the tough *little Sheila* part of me that I wanted them to see. I thought this was what respect was all about- physical strength and competitiveness. At least, that's what everybody told me it should be about for a body-builder, which is what I was expected to become. That's how it had always been with me. But, for some reason I couldn't explain, I had a funny feeling that things were about to change for me."

"How was that, Mrs. Palmer?" asked Detective Patterson.

"Well, for one thing, I was starting to notice how different I was from a lot of the women there in their *girly girl* outfits. I watched them in the locker room, helping each other put-on make up or fixing hair. I told myself that kind of stuff was stupid and that I didn't need their help. I was self-sufficient. We were there for different reasons. They were satisfied with any kind of attention, even if it was a demeaning or sexual remark. Those were cheap thrills, good for a minute but not meant to last. I told myself that being like them would not get me where I wanted to go. After all, I was serious about what I was doing and not some weekend warrior or exhibitionist looking for a casual date. The problem was that I was having to remind myself more often to keep up my tough girl persona. A part of me was starting to envy them, but I didn't know exactly why. I had a feeling that I wanted to be more like them than I admitted … that I had … a feminine side; but, even if I did I could never show it. I had to keep my guard up, wear a mask to maintain my reputation.

Reassured that my membership in the club with the guys was still intact, I fired back a sarcastic comment of my own. I said, 'Yeah, it must be jelly cause jam don't shake that way.' That got a good laugh out of everyone, proving that there were no hard feelings or misunderstandings on either side.

As usual, I was dressed in a baggy shirt and loose fitting work-out pants purposely designed to hide how fast my all-ready pumped muscles were developing. I wanted to keep my progress a secret until a few days before the competition. My muscles needed a good stretch. I obliged, then got ready to start my first bench-press routine. I wanted to finish as quickly as possible so I could go home and relax in a hot Epson-salt bath and listen to my music. Still recovering from my morning session, my goal was to do four sets, each with eight to ten repetitions. I put my gloves on and was just about to recline backwards and lift the bar above my chest when I felt the kind of body heat that comes when someone stands directly behind you."

"I sometimes do that to people when I go to the gym. Is that wrong?" asked Detective Patterson.

"There's no law against it," said Sheila. "But, it's an unspoken rule that we gym rats respect and it had just been broken. No one entered another person's space except by invitation. That was *my* space and no invitation had been extended. I prepared to start my count over from the beginning.

The hour was late and the air conditioner was struggling to keep the room cool. My face was wet with sweat and my body still ached from the morning session. It was not a time for fun and games. I wanted to give this intruder a piece of my mind. My pulse was racing. The muscles in my neck tensed with anger and I suspected that it would play-out in some major uncomfortable physical way. With my next breath, I felt what could only be the birth of a crick. I lowered the bar, making sure that it was locked and secured. Still reclining on the bench, I was just about to sit-up and turn around when I heard a honeyed, deep baritone voice say, 'I'm Thomas. I'll spot you.' I wondered if he was actually concerned about my welfare or just another creep looking for an easy date.

Little did I know that voice belonged to the man who was to become my ... husband."

Detective Patterson turned off the recorder. Only then did he notice the burned-out butt of his cigarette, still between his fingers. Dropping it into the ash tray, he stood up and said, "You're doing fine. Mrs. Palmer. I need to step-out for a few minutes. I've got another case going and some details I need to attend to. Would you mind if my partner takes over for a while? I'll be back as soon as I can. Detective Riley will be here shortly."

"Whatever you say, detective. Do I have to repeat anything?"

"No, everything so far is on tape. Just pick-up from where we stopped."

Chapter 6

Detective Patterson left the room, closing the door behind him. The payoff for his many years working homicide was that he was one of the highest ranking officers and a designated team leader. He understood that crimes were only puzzles to be solved - gather the facts, collect the evidence, make the arrest. A detective had to leave personal issues outside of the interrogation room, always keeping them separate from the suspects issues. His partner was new to the unit. Her work so far was adequate. But no one knew exactly why it was that she left her prior assignment. Was there anything that might compromise her performance on this case? He would watch her, assess her strengths and weaknesses, notice any sign of insecurity or loss of confidence. But, first things first. Take a quick bathroom break and then get into the observation room as carefully as possible. That room needed to be kept dark to hide his outline. Nothing must happen to violate department protocol.

Sheila sat alone, wondering what the next detective was going to be like. Had she made a mistake not asking for an attorney? All of her energy had been put into reading this one, discovering how to say things in a way that would make him sympathetic to her plight. Physically and emotionally drained, she wondered how much more she had left to give. She put her head down on the table and closed her eyes hoping to catch a quick nap before continuing with the questioning.

She was just starting to drift off to sleep, when the sudden hollow sound of knuckles rapping at the door woke her from her reverie.

Reluctantly Sheila sat up and was pleased to see that this new detective was a woman.

"Hello, I'm Detective Riley. I'm taking over for my partner. He went over your rights?" Like Sheila, the smell of smoke bothered her, but she had long sense learned to tolerate it. Being in smoke-filled rooms came with the job. Leaving the door ajar, she walked across the room and stood by the conference table.

"Yes, he did."

"Good. Heard that you had a rough night?"

They were strangers, but somehow Sheila felt that this one would appreciate her story in a way that Detective Patterson could never do. She was younger than her partner, possibly by several years. Her brown skin, accentuated by a minimum of makeup, appeared flawless. Her business casual attire, while the perfect choice to complement her prim and proper posture, was still a reminder of the authority and power she represented. Her auburn hair was carefully pulled back in a pony tail that dangled just above the collar of her crisp white shirt, buttoned all the way to the top, its long sleeves rolled-up just above her elbows. Her pumps were the same dark blue color as her skirt, with the hemline falling just above her knees. A shield was prominently displayed, along with her holstered service weapon and credentials hanging from a lanyard around her neck.

Sheila had to find a way to get this woman in her corner. "Please believe me. I know that what I'm saying sounds strange, but every word is true."

Detective Riley eyed her with a steady gaze. "Mrs. Palmer, you look like you're a smart cookie." Pointing to the mirror on the wall, she continued, "Look over there."

Seeing her point in his direction, Detective Patterson made a frantic attempt to send a mental message through the glass. *Don't tell her about the observation room.*

His message obviously not received, Detective Riley continued. "This is not a mirror. There is a room on the other side. I was sitting in that room, listening to everything you said."

Grimacing in disbelief, Detective Patterson thought, *Why the hell did she tell her that?*

The room having had sufficient time to air-out, Detective Riley walked back to the door, closed it, then walked over to the table. By the way that she carried herself it was obvious that she was a person not to be trifled with. "I promise you that I will keep an open mind." Sitting in a chair directly across from Sheila, she said, "I'm going to make a few notes." Reaching for a pen and one of the note pads on the table, she said, "The tape recorder is on. Please continue."

"Ok. Let's see. I was talking about the gym. It was when I sat-up and faced him, Thomas, that the crick in my neck became a distant memory. He was standing directly behind me, his grey work-out sweats fighting a losing battle to conceal his muscular body. My attention was immediately drawn to his eyes which were shark like, black and penetrating. Those eyes held me captive, locking me in a vice from which there seemed to be no escape. I couldn't say anything, let alone give him a tongue-lashing. I felt like those eyes were playing with me, testing me to see if I had what it took to break his spell. Satisfied that I couldn't, he smiled and quickly relaxed his gaze, seemingly amused by the whole thing.

That was ... unsettling. When my voice returned I said, 'Well, if it wouldn't be too much trouble for you. By the way, my name is Sheila.' I rarely talked to anyone during my workouts because I was always so focused. It was a mystery to me why it was so easy for those words to come from my mouth.

Thomas nodded but didn't say another word. I chalked that up to him being the silent type. I laid back down on the bench, raised the bar and started my repetitions. I kept wondering why he offered to help me."

"I wonder about that too," said Detective Riley, her brow furrowing. "That night was the first time you met him?"

"Yes... at least I think it was. That gym is a twenty-four hour business. A lot of people are in and out. Anyway, I don't remember seeing him before that night. The experience was unsettling to say the least. But, at the same time, there was something about it that intrigued me. Someone who actually knew his way around the gym was volunteering to watch over me and give me pointers. I plowed through the required sets, occasionally hearing him grunt or offer a word of encouragement. He kept an eye on me until I finished, hovering like some kind of self-appointed guardian. Some of the guys glanced in our direction but didn't say anything to him. His comments were direct and to the point. And, there was something else."

"What?" asked Detective Riley.

"His voice was mellow and dripping with honey and apparently I was more than ready to lick the spoon."

"Come again?" queried Detective Riley, apparently surprised by the comment.

"I wasn't used to being around anyone like that. Malik had changed so much over the years. The only feedback that I ever got from him was so negative. That was a definite turn-off. But this stranger puzzled me. He was … holding my attention."

"Oh, I see," said Detective Riley. Then what happened?"

"Well, this is going to get a little … graphic. I hope it won't offend you."

With a smug smile on her face, Detective Riley said, "Mrs. Palmer, let me explain something. I'm a police officer, specifically a Homicide Detective. I don't embarrass easily; so, please continue." *Good move, she's definitely got style*, thought Detective Patterson as he watched from the observation room.

"Well, the hour passed and my session ended. I thanked Thomas for his assistance and went to the locker room. Most of the women were still out on the main floor, so I almost had the entire place to myself. I decided to take a shower and stepped into a stall. That was the only place in the gym where I could let my guard down. I could just relax and get lost in the mist. I could take-off my mask - embrace my femininity without being concerned that prying eyes were watching for any sign of vulnerability. I reached for the handle and turned it to the warm setting. The water, initially calm, began to pulsate as it flowed down my body. Suddenly, I felt an energy surround me that was ... how can I put it, almost erotic in nature. Thoughts of Thomas began to intrude and I found myself wondering what it would be like to get to know him. What would I do if he walked in and got in the shower with me, pressed his hard body against mine, his hot breath on my neck, hands moving slowly over bodies pulsing together. Have you ever felt like that, Detective? Detective Riley?"

Chapter 7

The other detectives had a standing joke about Detective Riley. They called her *Starched Cakes* behind her back. She didn't socialize well with her coworkers in the break room, always sat at a table by herself, and never talked about her personal life. She had a reputation in the department for never showing her feelings or complaining about anything, especially about the temperature in the building. She usually found it quite comfortable, that is until now. Suddenly it felt like the heat had been turned-on sky high. The sweat beading up on her forehead, she began to undue the top buttons on her shirt. Evidently she forgot that her partner was sitting in the darkened observation room. Detective Patterson noticed little things that others considered insignificant. The tape recorder and the hidden camera would pick-up the interview details. Right now, his attention was focused on his partner and what she was doing with particular interest.

Turning off the tape-recorder, Detective Riley said, "Just a minute, Mrs. Palmer, I need to check something."

The thermostat was placed on the wall by the door. Detective Riley walked over to it, confirmed that it was set below seventy degrees, and walked back to her chair. *Why is it so hot in here?* Then she recognized where the heat was really coming from.

Detective Riley did not intend for it to happen, but she was beginning to feel wave-like flashes of intense heat coursing throughout her body. This conversation was actually turning her on. That rush of excitement was a familiar feeling, but it only happened at work when she was bored. Being bored wasn't what she expected when she was transferred to this unit. She spent the majority of her waking hours at work in her cubicle. With the exception of completing the mountain of paperwork cluttering her desk, no other duty had been assigned to date. That was not her idea of real detective work, but that's all she did, day after day.

Boredom came with downtime, especially between cases. Her co-workers relieved their boredom in the break-room - talking, joking and so on. When she walked in, the tension in the air grew stifling, making it obvious that her presence was not welcomed. It got worse as she moved up the career ladder. Taking her job seriously, she was reliable and her credentials were top-notch. True, she wasn't the best conversationalist, but neither was she a wall flower. To be social was her true nature, and like anyone else, she wanted to be accepted, welcomed, to feel like she belonged and had something of worth to offer.

What branded her an outsider and kept her from getting what she craved the most? Everything considered, the only conclusion was that it was her gender. She was a woman in a career area traditionally dominated by men. That was enough to merit their distain and therefore exclusion.

As hard of a pill as it was for her to swallow, rejection was something she had gotten used to. Lonely as she was, she had bills to pay. Not having hit rock bottom, she developed a survival tactic. She filled the void by "borrowing" details from her cases and using them to create her own fantasy world. At first it was just for amusement, then it became an addiction. Each detail became a little treasure, carefully recorded in a notebook, cleverly hidden in the top drawer of her desk. It was a cheap thrill, helped her get though the day, and a harmless vicarious mental diversion that harmed no one. If what Sheila had said was any indication of what was to come, then her statement would yield book material worth more than winning the state lottery.

Returning to the table, Detective Riley thought, *I'll have to remind myself to get more paper. The way this chick is going I'm sure to run-out before long.* Turning the microphone back on, she said, "Have I ever felt that way? I really couldn't say, Mrs. Palmer." The microphone was so sensitive that Detective Patterson clearly heard the sound of his partners breathing becoming slower and heavier. *Oh my God, she's losing it.* Had he known what was really happening with her, he would have made a bee line back into the room, then tactfully taken over. Otherwise, and given his lumbago, there was no reason for him to exert himself.

"Please continue," said Detective Riley.

"Ok. I drifted from fantasy to fantasy, each time gaining a new appreciation for the fragrance of lavender scenting the stream of water curling around me, touching every part of me. I was in there so long that the warm water began to run cold. My bubble burst, I made a quick exit, walked back into the locker room and started putting on my street clothes. There was no sense fooling myself. What did I have that would make me stand-out? I was definitely in the game, but there were so many beautiful women in the gym who went to great lengths to see how much skin they could get away with legally exposing. I didn't fit the profile in that respect. I told myself that I would never see Thomas again. My fantasies would have to do.

I put on my make-up, packed my gym bag and started walking back to the lobby. Imagine my surprise when I saw Thomas, leaning against the wall with his arms casually folded across his chest. I thought to myself, *Lord, this guy is hot stuff!* Apparently I wasn't the only woman in the room who felt that way. Women walked by him giving him stares that were more than just invitations. Not seeming to be interested, he tried to be cool, but I watched his eyes. They glowed with intensity as his gaze quickly darted back and forth, moving from face to face, trying not to be detected. He looked to be searching for someone in particular."

"Any idea as to who that might have been, Mrs. Palmer?"

"I'll give you one guess - me. He saw me coming and fixed his gaze on me like a magnet. There was no-doubt that I was the target of his hunt. *He was so fine! Mmm! Look out ladies. You're about to be one-upped by little Sheila!* His hair was black except for a few grey strands clustered around his temples. Well-trimmed, he still tried to run his fingers through the mass of kinky curls. He had obviously taken time to change into something that was definitely not gym wear. Straightening his posture, he had the look of a man set for a casual night out on the town. A pair of dark loafers replaced his white Air Jordan tennis shoes. His navy blue-colored jeans were just tight enough to hug his perfectly shaped butt and legs without setting off the fire alarm. A hint of a smile flashed across his face, confirming that he liked what he saw. I was overjoyed. My confidence level hit a new high. I walked toward him like he was my prince and I was Cinderella going to the ball.

Trying my best to appear indifferent, I said, 'You're still here? I thought that you would have been gone long ago.'

'No,' he said. 'Not until I found someone worth my time and effort to leave with. Would you like to get something to eat?' As if on cue, my stomach began to growl like it was begging me to accept his invitation. Dressed as he was, it never entered my mind that he would suggest that we go dutch treat. But, I decided to ask anyway, just to avoid any misunderstanding.

I said, 'I hope that it's on you. I never bring a lot of money to the gym.'

Trying not to come off as too patronizing, Thomas smiled politely and said, 'It's on me.'

I asked him if I was dressed ok for where we were going and he said, 'It will pass muster. Don't worry about it, this time.'

With that, I quickly accepted his offer. Actually, this man of mystery was already starting to work a powerful mojo on my mind. I was way past falling for him and wanted to learn his secrets. This dinner was the perfect opportunity."

Lost in the moment, Detective Riley said, "What happened next?"

"It was still early evening. The sweet fragrance of jasmine was starting to fill the air. We walked past several restaurants known to cater to gym folks watching their waist lines. Thomas ushered me into a small building I passed many times, but never entered. He opened the door for me and we walked into a smartly appointed reception area that connected to two larger rooms. It's not far from here. It's called, The Yellow Fin. Do you know the place, Detective Riley?"

"I don't think so, Mrs. Palmer." *Maybe I'll go there next week on my lunch break*, she thought, her fingers flying across the paper as she jotted-down the name.

"Tables and booths were draped with colorful cloths creating a tropical ambiance that was surprising, given the location. The place seemed almost too small for the long partition in the rear that hid a hallway leading to the restrooms and kitchen areas. It was near closing time but customers were still arriving, taking advantage of the late-night specials. I could see several waiters peeping from behind the partition. They were all dressed alike in dark pants, long-sleeved white button-down shirts and black ties. Suddenly one walked toward us. He appeared to be in his early twenties. What set him apart was his blonde hair neatly trimmed just above his shoulders, piercing brown eyes and deep-set dimples.

'How y'all doin? Party of two?' he drawled, while reaching into a container filled with well-worn menus.

Thomas raised an eyebrow, flashed a dazzling white smile and said, 'Table for two reserved for Mr. Thomas Palmer.' He was so sure of himself. But he was right. He made reservations while I dressed, knowing I wouldn't turn him down.

The waiter said, 'Of course, right this way, *Mr. Palmer.*' With that, he ushered us to a table tucked away in a secluded corner.

Thomas moved around the room with the air of a man used to frequenting such places. Walking to my side of the table, he pulled my chair out, and stood behind me until I sat down. He was so classy! Malik never acted that way. With him it was, 'Let's get a burger at McDonalds, you paying?' Assured that I was comfortable, Thomas walked to his chair, took-off his blazer and carefully ran his hands across the material to smooth-out any lingering wrinkles. All being in order, he hung it across the back and sat down. His grey shirt, unbuttoned from the collar to partly down his chest, was open just wide enough for me to see the braided gold chain hanging around his neck, tangled in a mass of closely cropped curly black hair.

The subdued lighting was intimate, but more than adequate to read the menu as the waiter pointed to different items.

'The lady will order first,' he said. I thought to myself, *He's talking about me!*

Not having much experience eating in such a fancy place, I wasn't sure what to order. So, I asked him what he would suggest. He said, 'Since you are in training, I suggest baked chicken with brown rice and broccoli. Oh yes, the lemon-butter sauce goes well with the broccoli.'

'Ok, that sounds fine,' I said, wondering how long it would take before I got used to this man taking care of me.

Thomas ordered the prime New York strip steak, medium well done, with mac and cheese. As an afterthought he told the waiter to bring him a gin and tonic. Without looking up from the menu, he asked me if I wanted a cocktail. I said 'No, just hot tea.' "

Trying her best to make a wisecrack, Detective Riley said, "Sounds like a world traveler?"

"Yeah, or something else, but I didn't find out what until later. Anyway, he acted like he didn't hear me. He told the waiter to forget the tea. Looking at me with his black eyes twinkling in the dim light, he said, 'Spoken like a non-drinker. I know something you'll love, something that goes with your ... personality, something that's *dark and stormy*.'

I asked him what was in it and he said, 'Oh, just a little rum, ginger beer, lime juice - more ice than anything else. Also, a mint garnish.' "

"And, what did you say?" asked Detective Riley.

"Well, he was already springing for dinner, and now a drink. That told me he was ... interested. I didn't want to look unsophisticated, so I said I would try it. The waiter took our order, then quickly turned and disappeared behind the partition."

Chapter 8

"Ok," said Detective Riley. " So now you're at the restaurant, placed your order and waiting for it to come back. How did you spend the down-time?"

Good summary, thought Detective Paterson.

"I was eager to start my investigation, so I began talking about the gym and how my work-outs were going. Thomas listened, asked for more information or made comments which were surprisingly perceptive and insightful. Things were just getting interesting when the waiter returned carrying a tray packed with steaming hot plates. He carefully placed them on our table, then stood nearby as we began eating. He looked nervous, shifting his weight from one foot to the other, until we said that everything was satisfactory. Then he smiled and left us to look out for customers at another table. We continued eating and talking about me until I saw an opportunity to change the direction of the conversation. I started asking Thomas questions about his background. Things had been so pleasant that I wasn't prepared for how that would bring our pleasant conversation to a standstill."

"What do you mean, Mrs. Palmer?" asked Detective Riley.

"He didn't want to answer my questions and asked me why I was so curious about him. He said, 'Look Sheila, I'm kind-of a private person. If there is something I want you to know, then I will tell you. Ok?'

That's what he said. He had an irritating smirk on his face, and I could tell that he was becoming bothered. At that moment he reminded me of Malik and it scared me. I told myself that I would have to be more careful, maybe try to second-guess what might anger him, or else something bad might happen to me."

"That's quite a comparison, Mrs. Palmer," said Detective Riley. *I wonder if he was into rough sex? That's a definite turn-on. Hope she brings it up.* "Was that the only reason you thought that he might harm you?"

"No, I just had a feeling. I tried to smooth it over, telling him that since we talked so much about me I figured he might want equal time. Then, without warning, he slid his chair so close to me that there was barely any space between us. I felt his cheek brush against mine as he placed his arm on the back of my chair. It was kinda disgusting because the scent of undigested meat hit me square in the face."

Detective Riley momentarily forgot about maintaining a professional demeanor. She felt herself becoming captivated by the story this suspect was telling. In fact, she looked more like a groupie, elbows on the table, head propped-up in her hands. There was one question she was absolutely dying to ask. But doing so would violate sanctioned department protocol regarding conducting investigations and maybe blow the case. She decided to take the conservative route, but the look on her face told Detective Patterson that his partner had something on her mind that was driving her crazy.

"Then what happened?" she asked.

"Thomas said something that almost blew my mind. He said, 'Trust me, learning about you is more interesting to me than you can imagine.' His tone was so menacing that it made me sit in stunned silence. He said, 'I want to ask you something. Are you really happy with who you are?' "

"What was your answer, Mrs. Palmer?"

"I was trying not to choke on the small bit of food in my mouth. His black eyes narrowed, almost to slits, giving me a look that seemed to cut right through my body. I said, 'Uh ... that's an interesting question. Let me think about it for a moment.' I decided to sip my cocktail as a distraction. The sweet delicious taste rolled over my tongue and down my throat like warm syrup. I took another sip and reminded myself not to gulp it all down at once.

Since I didn't totally shut him down, Thomas decided to go for broke. This time, his tone was more ... cordial.

'Everyone wears a mask,' he said. *How did he know?* 'I want to see who's behind yours. I want to get to know the real you. Are you afraid about something? You seem so... lonely. It's just a feeling, but you seem to be carrying around a lot of baggage - so stressed-out. Is it the gym? Maybe I can help?'

I asked him why he wanted to help me. His answer was that he had his reasons. Then he slid his chair back to the other side of the table and continued

44

eating. I didn't know what to say, so he asked me if he had hit a nerve and told me to take all the time I needed before answering."

Detective Riley tapped her pen on the table. Something Sheila said annoyed her and she didn't know why. "So he sensed that you had some concerns about what he was asking?"

"He must have. I didn't like his arrogance, the smugness in his voice. I took a deep breath and tried to mock his matter-of-fact tone. I said, 'Of course, I … love … me.'

My answer didn't go over well with him. He sighed, then after a few seconds said, 'Let's get real. I'll tell you what I think. You act so - stuck-up, not as much as some I know, but enough. Living like that's got to be … stressful. Is that who you really are, or is that what you try to act like? You know, people wear masks for different reasons - pride, insecurity, fear, … past mistakes. Frankly, I don' t see you as the type that would have those kinds of issues. But, what do I know. I'm not part of the gym staff, and I'm not training to get on anybody's stage in a speedo.' "

Momentarily frustrated by her inability to solve the puzzle swirling around in her head, Detective Riley asked, "And, what was your reaction?"

"My feelings were all mixed up. *How could I want him and find him disgusting at the same time?* What if I did have issues? Didn't everyone have issues? And, calling me stuck-up was like the pot calling the kettle black! I barely knew him. What right did he have to ask me to air all of my dirty linen and in that place? On the other hand, caustic as his words were, they did

45

hit home. People said that it was easier to talk about such things with a stranger. So, what the hell.....

I tried to think carefully before answering. I decided to be honest with him. I'll never forget what I told him. 'You are the first person who has ever asked me that. Since you want to know, I'll tell you. Have you ever been afraid of... loss and rejection? Well I have, my whole life. That fear has made me what I am today. Lonely? Yes... I've done everything on my own, never looking for a handout or a hand-up. Stress? Yes, I've known stress. I've lived with it my whole life. First, my parents dreamed a dream for me - then I chose their dream, made it my own and wanted to be perfect at it - looks, actions, goals, the whole nine yards. I thought that's what it would take to keep them ... loving me. I didn't want to rock the boat because I was ... safe. But the price was high. I never got to know ... the real me, what I wanted. The gym, that's a laugh. I'm in pain every night, especially when I lift those heavy weights. And I can never complain because the guys will think I'm weak and I'll lose their respect. They might - reject me. I'm around all those pretty women in their *girly girl* get-ups, looking like crap. My hair gets messed up, I get all sweaty and I can't wait to get out of there. But, I have a reputation to maintain and trying to change things right now would complicate my life too much. So I just keep on doing what I'm doing, wearing my mask.' "

That was it. Detective Riley couldn't believe how similar some of the issues in Sheila's disclosure were to those in her own life. She knew what it felt like to go through that kind of fear, loneliness, deception, … rejection.

She knew that kind of … pain. While sympathetic with her plight, she had to find a way to distance herself, remain objective. She could not afford for this woman to see her as an ally. Gathering her composure, she asked, "And, how did you feel after making that disclosure?"

" … vulnerable, naked, stripped of my defenses. I could feel him reading me, trying to see past my words, learning where my true weaknesses were. I sensed that he enjoyed my rant, maybe even felt … superior for having made it happen, and I kicked myself for being such a fool, willingly providing this information, not knowing what use he might put it to. I felt tired, like I was on the losing side of some kind of war that I didn't start or know how to win. I realized that I would never be the same. My mask was off, now what was I supposed to do? Not only had I just admitted that I was living a lie but that I hated myself for doing it, wanted to change, but didn't know how or even if I could. The food I was chewing suddenly lost its taste. The conversation had become way too heavy.

Thomas never blinked the whole time I was talking. Then, to my surprise, he laughed and said, 'See, I was right. I knew something was up. Thanks for the honesty. Bye the way, if you don't already know it, I think you're really something special! If you were mine, you'd always be … safe.' I was flattered by his words but his tone was … patronizing. The hour was late. I was tired, a little tipsy, and had no intention of saying anything more that might cause conflict. I smiled and continued eating, telling myself that I had no right to be upset with him. I hardly knew him, but I was already in love with him. He just wanted to help me rise to a higher level. I vowed to hold him to his offer."

Chapter 9

The interview was progressing nicely, but Detective Riley hoped that the conversation would take a more *sensual* direction. Little did she know that her wish was about to be granted. She looked at Sheila and said, "What came-out of that conversation at the restaurant?"

"Well, I felt he respected me for what I said. It also helped to break the ice. Thomas became less defensive and carried the conversation while I ate the rest of my food, which by then was quite cold. Having more than a superficial relationship with him was suddenly a real possibility. And, I hoped that the feeling was mutual.

It was then that he started talking about his background. He also grew-up in Fifth Ward Houston, not far from where I lived. He even said that he passed my house many times when visiting friends. He had a rough childhood. His family was poor, so after graduating from high school, he went into the Army and did well for himself. He did tours in Germany and the Philippines, got all the way up to Lieutenant Colonel and was even a staff officer. But then he developed a medical condition, something about his heart, nothing big but enough to get him a general discharge with benefits. He was in a motorcycle accident a few months ago which was why he was in the gym. He blew his knee out and had to have replacement surgery. Working-out was his physical therapy. It was painful but the doctors told him that it would get better with time.

Up until then we hadn't talked about our age difference. Except for the grey in his hair and his sophisticated ways, he didn't seem that much older than I was. But when I asked, his hesitation told me that there might be some concern about how I would take his response. His recovery was smooth. He leaned toward me and with a sly smile said, 'I'm forty-five.' Once again, the conversation had suddenly become awkward.

I guess he sensed my concern because he asked me if I had a problem being seen with an older man. His black eyes narrowed as he studied my face, searching for any sign of rejection or hesitancy. He was right on target. My feelings were all mixed up. My heart was whispering *cast your fate to the wind and go for it*. My mind was screaming at me that I needed to get out of there in a hurry. This age difference opened-up a whole new can of worms. He was about the same age as my father and we certainly didn't see eye-to-eye on a whole bunch of topics. If we married, could that generation gap lead to misunderstandings?

Then there were medical issues which, considering the age difference, were known and sure to arise. On the other hand, Thomas was in pretty good shape for a man of his age. That definitely worked in his favor. In fact, he had the athletic physique of a stone-cold fox who could easily pass for a rock-star! I guessed him to be over six feet tall. The definition of his broad shoulders and six-pack abs pressed against his grey form-fitting shirt. A neatly trimmed mustache served as the perfect frame for lips that begged to be kissed. His creamy dark- brown skin seemed to accentuate the veins criss-crossing his arm muscles, almost like they were popping, especially when he flexed."

Satisfied with how things were beginning to pick-up, Detective Riley smiled and said, "So, you followed your heart."

"Yeah, there was always the possibility of a lived-happily-ever-after scenario."

Stone-cold fox, broad shoulders, six-pack abs, form-fitting shirt, kissable lips, popping veins …Detective Riley smiled and said, "Please continue."

"We sat in that restaurant and talked until the waiter came over to our table with the bill. Thomas pulled-out a wad of what looked like hundred dollar bills. He peeled-off two of them and said, 'This is for the bill -keep the change, and here's a little something extra for your service.' He gave the guy a hundred-dollar tip. The meal only cost sixty dollars, including the drinks. That waiter almost passed-out!"

Now that's the kind of man I'm talking about! thought Detective Riley.

"The hour was late and few busses were still in service. I was grateful when Thomas offered to drive me home. We started walking the short distance to the parking lot next to the gym. It was still muggy and hot, and the air was heavy with the scent of jasmine. Still slightly buzzed from my cocktail, I didn't protest when he moved closer to me and put his arm around my shoulder."

"And, then?" asked Detective Riley.

"Reaching the parking lot, I noticed that one car stood out from the others. It reminded me of a sleek, sophisticated racing sports car, the kind that's made for two people. I have a thing for cars like that, so I didn't hold back my approval. Thomas told me it was a vintage, Mercedes, SL-Class, just a little something he picked-up while overseas. The car's silver finish gleamed brighter than the security lights in the lot. He clicked the remote door opener, walked ahead of me and was standing by the passenger side when I got there, patiently waiting for my arrival. I peeped in as the door opened and marveled at how the soft amber glow gave the dashboard an otherworldly feeling. Filled with knobs of various shapes and sizes, it's complicated look was of no concern to him. Reaching beyond me into the car, one wave of his hand sent the sultry crooning voice of Marvin Gaye gliding around my head like a silk scarf … *"Since I had you girl I haven't wanted any other lover."* Then he pulled me close into his embrace and we danced. I didn't care that the security cameras were recording our every move. The smell of his cologne mixing with the crisp clean freshness of his shirt intensified what was already a hypnotic spell. His hands moving up and down my spine created a tension between us that flared-up like a bonfire. The piece ended and he reached for my hand, walked me back to the car, waited until I was seated, then adjusted the headrest for my comfort. The tanned leather bucket seats still had that new car smell. Without hesitation, I settled back and surrendered to an ambiance of pure sensuality."

"Sounds like a hot number. I'd like to take a ride in that one myself," sighed Detective Riley. Still observing from the observation room, Detective Patterson felt the hairs on the back of his neck beginning to stand up. *Whoa...What's that about?* His decision was made. *I'll give her five more minutes, then I'm going in.*

"So what happened next, Mrs. Palmer?"

"As he drove, the way that he handled that stickshift was almost graceful, like a band leader waving a baton. He put the top down and I saw the city lights whizzing by, unable to compete with the canopy of stars hovering above us."

Struggling to maintain a detached demeanor, Detective Riley sat on the edge of her chair, spellbound, never imaging that an interrogation could be interesting and arousing at the same time. That Marvin Gaye cut was one of her favorite songs and now it played in her head like a worm burrowing deep into an apple. The material she was getting from Sheila's statement would fuel her fantasies for months to come!

Hoping to put the icing on the cake, Detective Riley fished for more details. "Did he try to make a pass?"

"Yeah, he did, and actually anything could have happened. But, it didn't."

"Oh," groaned Detective Riley, shrugging her shoulders in disappointment. Her response did not go unnoticed by her partner.

Smiling, Sheila continued, "He told me that his apartment wasn't far and invited me over for another ... cocktail. His hidden agenda was obvious. I'm not easy but I still wanted to dangle a carrot in front of him. So I said, 'Maybe next time.' "

"Did he take that as rejection?" asked Detective Riley.

"Not at all. In fact he told me that he would count on it."

Chapter 10

Detective Patterson considered himself to be a fair-minded man. His partner was a Homicide Detective, trained and licensed but not seasoned. Was her lack of experience why he foresaw trouble headed her way? He had a talent for knowing such things. His nose would twitch, a strange habit, one that he rarely talked about but was almost one-hundred percent accurate. And it was happening now. If she had issues, he hoped that they weren't interfering with her professional responsibility. As the senior team member, it was his duty to not let her fail. He just had to dig deeper, uncover the hidden truth before it could do damage.

Never one to gossip, he avoided going into the department break room just for that reason. That kind of talk was petty and usually without merit. But, maybe this time, their questions were justified. There was always more to a story than met the eye. Was his partner hiding something? Maybe she was leading a double life, but why? He knew enough about human nature to understand that still waters could run deep. One thing was for sure. Mrs. Palmer was saying things that triggered something in Detective Riley's personal life. But what was the connection? An interesting story festered underneath his partner's calm exterior and he intended to bring it to light.

Rushing to get back into the interrogation room, he almost tripped over a chair in the hallway next to the door.

The tape recorder was still running when he walked in. "Sorry that it took so long for me to get back. Detective Riley, how are things going?"

"So far, so good, Detective Patterson."

"Glad to hear it. I'll listen to the tape and catch-up later. Well, let's continue."

Detective Patterson made himself comfortable in one of the cushioned chairs. Assuming a professional posture, Detective Riley said, "Ok, Mrs. Palmer. Let's pick-up the next day when you got to the gym."

"Sure. You know, it's funny how quickly word gets around at the gym. The next day Malik was waiting for me. And, he was on time for a change. He started giving me the third degree and asked, 'What's up with you and this Thomas dude?'

I turned around and came face to face with a side of him I'd never seen before. Acting as nonchalant as possible, I said 'Oh, hi Malik, where have you been hiding yourself?' He snapped back at me. These were his exact words, 'You heard what I said. We have history. I thought you were *my* lady. I thought we were a couple.' He stood there, pursing his lips, his hooded hazel eyes now wide with indignation. But underneath that pretense of stoicism, I knew that he was just play acting. He was causing a scene and I didn't want to do anything to put my gym membership in jeopardy. It was obvious that he wasn't going to be put-off that easily.

I said, 'Your lady? Whatever gave you that impression? That puppy-dog crush I had on you when we were kids has been long gone. You were just helping me out as a training partner. That's all. But since you brought it up, I no longer need your assistance.'

Then his voice got kind of apologetic. He said, 'Ok, I know what's pissing you off. So I missed *one* session. I *really* had car trouble. What's the big deal?'

Minimizing my feelings like that did not win him any brownie points. I was tired of his mess. It was a perfect opportunity to end our association. Then he said, 'So, that's it, huh? This guy helps you out for one session and you're ready to kick me to the curb?'

I told him that it wasn't just that. We had different goals in life and always would. But, I wasn't about to tell him about the dinner. Frankly it wasn't his business. I offered to still be friends, but he said, 'Are you serious? You don't want to work with me anymore? Well, ok, if that's the way you want it. You'll be sorry. And remember, you'll always be *my* lady.' He turned to walk away, then suddenly spun around and said, 'Just watch your back, you .....' He grabbed his gym bag and stormed out of the gym, muttering something that caught the attention of the security guard standing by the exit. I didn't hear his exact words. "

Detective Patterson had been quietly tapping his shoe against one leg of the chair. It was getting late and his lumbago was really bothering him. Tapping his shoe was a way to take his mind off the pain and stay focused.

"Did you consider that a threat?" he asked.

"Actually no. More like being nasty. He didn't like what he heard and pitched a fit. The only thing that bothered me was when he told me to watch my back, know what I mean?"

Both Detectives nodded their heads in unison. "Can you think of anyone who possibly overheard the conversation?" asked Detective Patterson.

"No, there were so many people there, I couldn't pick-out anyone in particular. I'm sorry. But, I turned around and was surprised to see Thomas glaring at Malik, his black eyes huge and shark-like, empty, and very cold. I was surprised that he hadn't said anything. I asked him how long he had been standing there. His voice was low and reminded me of the rumbling of distant thunder. He said it was long enough. Actually he had been at the gym all evening, waiting for me. I was surprised that he didn't speak up. Then he asked me if I was ok. I said that I was, as long as he was nearby." Sheila rubbed her eyes which were starting to fill with tears. "Thomas smiled and told me that he wasn't going anywhere. His black eyes were dancing like flames in a candle."

Detective Patterson slowly shook his head. "It sounds like Thomas might have overheard the entire conversation. It's too bad that he's not here to back-up your account. "

Chapter 11

Detective Patterson could never imagine Sheila being at a loss for words. But he could envision a person getting lost in her words, if not careful.

"If you don't mind, I'd like for you to jump-ahead," he said. "It sounds like the way was clear for you and Thomas to get together, seeing as how Malik was out of the picture?"

"Yes, true enough," said Sheila. " I thought that Thomas would be my ticket out of loneliness. We worked-out together, days becoming weeks. I actually began to enjoy helping him more with his therapy than doing my own training exercises. Excited about the possibilities, I forgot about Maliks' warning. My mind was on the future, about how magical our union was going to be. Little did I imagine the darkness to come.

It wasn't long before Thomas became my lover, confidant, mentor and best friend. The attention he gave me was great and I was the envy of the other women at the gym. I was still tough *little Sheila* but was finding ways to embrace my femininity at the same time. So much about my mystery man was starting to come to light, or so I thought. He was good at financial matters and especially budgeting. As a matter of fact, we talked a lot about money management. Hell, he owned a Mercedes SL and lived in an up-scale part of town that I couldn't afford. That's why I didn't object when he volunteered to help me keep track of my finances. Dealing with the details stressed me out too much, so I was glad to let him handle it for me. He said that it was his way of paying me back for helping him at the gym. Of course that meant that I would have to give him access to my banking information."

"That was ... risky, wasn't it? What if he turned out to be a scammer?" asked Detective Patterson.

"Yes, but I didn't know anyone who had ever been scammed by another African American. Back then I didn't think twice. Now, I know better. There are rotten apples in all races, all age groups, and all genders. Plus, I was in *love*, living in my own little fantasy world, and wanted to show Thomas that he had my complete trust. Anyway, as far as I knew he hadn't done anything to raise a red flag."

"And do you think that he appreciated what you were doing for him?" asked Detective Riley.

"I like to think so. His rehabilitation was progressing and it was wonderful that he could finally laugh and get some relief from the chronic pain that had plagued him for so long."

Detective Patterson was steadily tapping his foot against his chair leg. Craving another cigarette, he reached into his pocket and took-out the package. Rubbing the smooth surface between his thumb and forefinger finger was comforting. Lighting-up, he took a long drag, exhaled the smoke and continued the interview. "Mrs. Palmer, it sounds like both of those men were ... stalking you, watching you, getting information about what to do or say to make you react in a certain way."

"Yes, I know that now. The goal was the same but the methods differed. Back then I honestly didn't understand what was really going on. Malik and Thomas were into using power and control to manipulate people. Both searched for my flaws then looked for opportunities to use them to get something from me. Malik was in-your-face, like "do-it-because-I-say-so." Thomas was … subtle. Take my bank account, for example. Thomas tried to make me believe that he was doing me a favor by letting him take over; but, what he really wanted was for me to trust him so much that he could use it as he pleased."

Detective Patterson wanted to be tactful when asking his next question. Hoping to avoid turning the interrogation into a therapy session, he asked, "Why do you think they picked you as their target? Convenience? Maybe they thought you were weak or naive?"

"Maybe," said Sheila, "but, the best laid-plans can turn around on you in a minute, especially because God don't like ugly. I think they came into my life for a reason - there was something I needed to learn and change about myself so that I could … mature, become a woman with a new attitude. Helping other people wasn't something I was brought-up to do…allowing myself to be controlled and used by them was. No one in my life had ever really been kind to me out of the goodness of their heart, and I rarely put myself out to help anyone, that is, before Thomas. With Thomas … I helped him not because I had to but because I loved him and wanted him to get better.

It was genuine, not fake. It made me feel like … it's hard to explain… like there was a whole new part of me that I was finally being introduced to, something that was beautiful and powerful and could be used for the betterment of someone besides myself. I really had a caring nature! The more I showed it, the better it felt. I made up my mind that if doing good for someone else moved me in that way, then that was how I wanted others to treat me. I deserved no less. Yes, that's it … I felt *empowered* … my life was finally changing for the better and I loved it. I was even ready to admit some hard truths about myself and take responsibility for the unpleasant consequences I brought upon myself. Lord knows, if this was going to help me earn good karma, then I was all in for it!

You know, Thomas was the one who said that he wanted to see what was behind the mask I wore. As devious as he could be, there were times when he seemed to be at war with himself to keep up that dark front. I believe that there is some good in everyone and maybe, for whatever reason, that was what he was trying to keep a lid on. But, he wasn't successful all the time. I believe that I saw that good part of him and that helped me look past the bad stuff. I'd like to believe that at some point he would have realized his plans were falling far short of his expectation. That would have thrown him for a loop. Maybe that would have been enough to make him change his ways - let his light shine through. If not …if he wanted to keep on taking the low road, then I'm sure he would have come-up with another manipulative approach. Anyhow, I was living in a fantasy world most of the time. The only thing on my mind was that what I saw as true happiness was within my reach and I was going to fight for it.

Interestingly enough, the guys at the gym seemed to like the *new* me. I guess what they say is true- you can catch more flies with honey than with vinegar. But as my popularity increased at the gym, Thomas grew more distant. He started acting a lot different toward me than when we first met."

"How was that, Mrs. Palmer?" asked Detective Patterson.

"He seemed jealous of the attention I was getting and how my life was turning around. I wasn't acting as he expected. It was rare that he complemented me about anything. But he wanted me to meet his needs without complaint or question. He seemed to feel like he was entitled to get all that I could give and stopped thanking me for the help I was giving him. That hurt my pride. I wondered if what I thought was love was really … infatuation.

He could be kind, but also brutally frank with what he had to say, sometimes without regard for how others would take it. We started arguing about little things. He blamed me for everything that went wrong and wouldn't stop until I agreed with him. Going along with him didn't fit the profile of the new woman I was becoming but it did keep the peace, at least for a while. Then I started finding reasons to excuse what he was doing. Maybe he was having second thoughts about us being together and didn't know how to tell me. Things were going from bad to worse. I felt what we initially had was slipping away. Why couldn't he be happy for me? I knew that he saw the change in my behavior. I decided that we needed to talk, clear the air. Know what I mean?"

"So what happened then?" asked Detective Riley.

"I saw an opening one day while we were at his apartment. We were sitting on his living room sofa, talking about something insignificant, when I told him how I felt. He listened without interruption, then to my surprise, moved closer to me. His body heat intensified the woody musk scent of his cologne and I felt that same old feeling coming back ..."

"Mrs. Palmer is all of this really necessary?" asked Detective Patterson.

It had been a while since Sheila had given Detective Riley anything worth saving for her private fantasies. Now that the faucet was turned on, she was not about to let her partner interrupt the flow. Before Sheila could answer, she said, "If she feels that it is, then it must be."

Wanting to present a unified front, Detective Patterson gave in. *My partner's got spunk. Let's see where this goes.* "Ok, ok, go ahead Mrs. Palmer."

"Well wouldn't you know it - he took the wind right out of my sail! It felt so good to once again feel the steady beat of his heart and the warmth of his embrace. He kissed my lips, gently, as if to put to rest any fears that I might have. His voice was just above a whisper as he said, 'Sheila, I want to tell you how much being with you these past few weeks has meant to me. I know how rough it has been for you to juggle your training schedule and also help me, and I ... will never forget it. You were unhappy with the life you had before we met. But it was the path you chose and my coming into it upset the balance. Anyway, I know that things are going to work out for... us.'

'Us, what's with this us?' I asked, trying my best to seem surprised, but loving every moment of what I thought his words implied.

'Well,' he continued, 'There was me and you, now there's ... us.'

'Oh,' I said. 'You mean, we are a team?'

Sighing with relief, he smiled and said, 'Yes, honey, just the way you put it.'

Every complaint I had was forgotten when I heard those words. In fact, I actually thanked God for bringing this man into my life. Then he said, 'Since you brought it up, yes, I noticed the change in you. It's ... good; but, be careful. What we have now is fragile. We have to take care of our team, guard it so it will endure. We have to get rid of anything that might work against us.' "

For a moment, Detective Patterson thought he saw his partner's eyes become moist with tears.

"Yes," said Detective Riley. "I can see where being considered part of a team would make you feel special - important, like you're... needed."

Chalking it up to the hazy effect from the overhead fluorescent lighting, Detective Patterson said, "Sounded like a warning. Did he tell you what his concern was?"

"No, I asked him, but he didn't go into detail. He did say something else that I didn't understand."

"What was that, Mrs. Palmer?"

"He stood up, repeatedly shifted his body weight from one foot to the another, and said, 'What I mean is ...you've worked so hard and all by yourself. Well, your lonely days are gone. I know how much you want to compete. Always remember that I'll be around, no matter what you decide to do. I want you to think carefully before making decisions on your own ... about anything. Just tell me what's on your mind before you make a move. Life can hold some interesting twists and turns, sometimes not what you planned or expected. You've got to be prepared to deal with whatever comes your way. I'll always be ... in your life, to guide you, protect you.' "

"That's interesting. Any idea what he meant?" asked Detective Patterson.

"At the time, no. I heard what I wanted to hear. When he said "around," I heard "in your life, watching your back, and you can come back to it in the future." And frankly speaking I was getting tired of double duty - my training and his therapy. It would be easier for me to put my competition plans on hold, but I had to be sure that he would be in my corner if I decided to revisit competition plans. I told him I wanted to stop my training."

"How did he take it?" asked Detective Riley.

"Better than I expected. I had reached a plateau and he knew that I had a steady job making big bucks as a fashion designer. We had separate apartments, but I ended up spending more time at his place. That's when I discovered just how vain he was, not only about his looks but about how he wanted me to look. I had to dress a certain way for my job, which was not necessarily the look he wanted me to have. I also wanted to please him and sometimes the pressure really got to me. Maybe there was a generation gap. He loved it when people said that *father time* had been good to him or asked if I was his daughter. People say that couples sometimes grow to resemble each other, so I could see how they might think we were blood relatives. I just ignored them. Sometimes, just for kicks, I would give him a quick kiss on the lips, a pat on his butt, and count the seconds of awkward silence until that stranger figured it out.

We had our differences but I felt we could work through them. Take food, for example. Even though I wasn't great in the kitchen, he politely ate what I cooked. But I could tell that he craved variety. So, we often ate-out and usually found ourselves back at the same strip-mall restaurant where we shared our first dinner. One night when we were there, Thomas ordered the Southern combo- spare-ribs, coleslaw, and corn bread, with apple cobbler as desert. I wasn't in training; however, I still found it difficult to steer clear of my old habits. So, I ordered salmon with asparagus."

Desperately wanting to pick up the pace, Detective Patterson groaned, "Mrs. Palmer, I...."

"Ok, I'll speed it up."

The waiter brought our food, still hot and steaming from the oven. We were joking and laughing, reviewing events of the day as usual. Then, suddenly the tone of the conversation became, somber. Yes, that's it, somber.

'Sheila,' he said, 'I'm a lot older than you are. You know, the day may come when I'm not going to be here.'

Knowing what he was leading up to, I guess he saw the sadness in my face. His voice got real soft, kinda like a father talking to his child. He said, 'No matter where I go, I'll always find a way to help you, to protect you. If you get into a jam, just call my name. And, listen to that little voice deep inside your gut before you act.' His eyes filled with tears. I had to look away because I couldn't stand to see him like that. I tried to joke it off by changing the subject, saying that day was a long way off, for both of us. I reminded him that there was something he wanted to ask me. I could feel my excitement mounting and was sure that I knew the answer to my own question.

'Yes,' he said, 'but I have something to ask you before I do that. Do you believe in … twin flames, life after death, that sort of stuff?'

The detectives looked at each other, trying to confirm that they were hearing the same thing. Detective Riley was the first to speak. "Excuse me, Mrs. Palmer?"

"You heard me right. He studied my face, trying to read my expression. My silence must have told him that I had no idea what he was talking about, so he said that we could discuss it another day. By the way, he also said that it was time that we move in together."

"What did you say?" asked Detective Riley.

"Hallelujah!"

Chapter 12

This time it was Detective Riley who asked to take a short break.

"We've been at this for a while. I'm going to step-out for a few minutes. Can I bring you anything back, Mrs. Palmer? A sandwich or some coffee?"

"Yes, I would love a cup of coffee, black, no sugar, thanks."

"Nothing for me, thanks," said Detective Patterson.

"No problem," said Detective Riley as she left the room, shutting the door behind her. That excuse gave her an opportunity to make a quick stop at her desk. Once seated, she casually opened the top drawer and took out her journal. The coffee could wait. She wanted to capture a few highlights before they were forgotten but couldn't chance her partner seeing her leave the room with her note pad. Her mission completed, she took a quick bathroom break then made her way to the break room to get the coffee. Returning to the interrogation room, she put the coffee on the table in front of Sheila and began listening to the interview in progress.

Detective Patterson had already kicked his questioning into high gear when she returned. It wasn't often that a case this involved presented itself. He was glad to be working with Detective Riley. The unit saddled her with paper-pushing tasks offering no opportunity for her to hone skills, let alone be observed while doing it. He heard that her credentials were above reproach, but a person could not rest on their laurels. He needed to see her in action so he could spread the word. That was the way to gain ... respect. Not knowing how she reacted to things, it was hard for him to clue into her mental processing. Every detective had issues, and it would do her good to see how well he kept his focus alert and in the here and now. He also reminded himself to demonstrate how to use a simple trick, a quick kind of honesty screening not necessarily known by the others in his unit. His years working homicide taught him how to detect a hand movement or change in voice tone that might signal an outright lie or discrepancy. In fact, he would use it without giving her advance notice. Skilled as he was, he would be able to tell if she recognized what he was doing.

As long-winded and tedious as her statement had been to that point, Detective Patterson hoped that Sheila was finally getting to the meat of her story. But she was nowhere close to being finished. "We decided that I would move in with him since his place was a lot larger than mine."

Detective Patterson was looking right at her. He saw her gaze shift suddenly, become unfocused and fall on a point somewhere beyond him. "Remember that fantasy I had when I was taking a shower at the gym that night Thomas and I met? Oh, that's right, you weren't in here when I talked about it. It's on the tape. Well, now I was living that fantasy."

Sitting in the observation room, Detective Patterson had heard every word. "And was it all you envisioned?" he asked.

Detective Riley noticed the blush rising to Sheila's cheeks. Surprised that she could feel so embarrassed, Sheila lowered her eyes and said, "Not entirely."

Being at a loss for words, Detective Patterson decided to take the easy way out. He smiled, reached for another cigarette and continued writing.

"It wasn't long before Thomas asked me to marry him. The news got back to the gym in record breaking time. One of my friends who was there told me what happened almost word for word. It went something like this…

The guys were standing in a group when Malik walked in. One of them said, 'Hey Malik, did you hear the news?'

Malik said, 'What news?'

'Remember that night you didn't show and how upset you got when Sheila let you go?'

'Yeah, so what?'

'Remember that guy who helped her out?'
'Yeah.....'

'Well, *little Shelia* is getting married to him.'

She said Malik pitched a fit right there, started cursing and throwing weights around and everything! Security came over and asked him to leave."

"The incident was probably recorded in their daily log. I'll check it out," said Detective Riley.

"I laughed when she told me. Anyway, I was so happy about getting married to Thomas! We decided to remain in Houston, mainly because we both had history here. When the time came to buy a house,

Thomas told me not to worry. He said that he had money in a bank account from something he did overseas, and ..."

"Did he say what that was, Mrs. Palmer?" asked Detective Patterson.

"No ... but that money, together with a loan from the VA, and what was in my account, would do the trick. That's when I found out that my decision to give him access to my finances was his way of putting my trust in him to the test. Had I refused, he would have just ... walked away, emotionally and then physically. Sometimes I wondered what he valued more, money or me.

Anyway, we got a really good deal on a two-story track home in the Third Ward, not far from the University. It wasn't cheap, so I probably should have paid more attention to how it was being financed. But I didn't. Word of our move got back to the gym in record breaking time. I wasn't too happy about that."

"Why was that, Mrs. Palmer?" asked Detective Patterson.

"Because I didn't want Malik to find out where we were living. I felt that we should keep our personal business to ourselves. Some people find out what you have and then play-up to you to see what they can get from you. Well, some of those guys were like that. They started coming over to our house and Thomas fell right into their trap. He wouldn't listen to me. He liked to brag and didn't know when to keep his mouth closed."

"Did being married change your husband's attitude toward you?" asked Detective Riley. Detective

Patterson looked at his partner and thought, *Good question, relevant and to the point.*

"Yes, but by then I had cut-back on my time at the gym and so had Thomas. He became the focus of my life and I was completely devoted to him. I wasn't competing anymore because I needed to concentrate on our home and his therapy. Besides, I didn't want to run into Malik. Thomas' rehabilitation from knee surgery was going great and we didn't have to worry about the money. His military health insurance paid for a physical therapist to come to our home which took some of the pressure off of me. I was concerned that dealing with therapy and the drama around all those guys was too much for him to handle."

"How so, Mrs. Palmer?" asked Detective Patterson.

"Well, his general health was starting to deteriorate. Let me back up for a minute. I grew up believing that the key to making a relationship last was a solid foundation built on love, intimacy, mutual respect and most importantly, trust. I did everything I could to make that happen for us. Thomas was everything to me. I fussed over him, maybe sometimes too much for his liking. He was quick to let me know when I was crowding him and I would give him space.

We didn't always have the same game plan as to how to stay healthy, but we both knew that it was important. I made the medical appointments and monitored medications. We were no different than anyone else. Sometimes we came down with colds or the flu, nothing that couldn't be fixed.

Thomas was basically a man's man. He didn't think that it was masculine to admit that he was in pain, so he rarely complained until he was just flat on his back. I really couldn't blame him because neither of us trusted what went on in hospitals. In fact, we avoided hospitals and doctors like the plague. Too many of our friends left hospitals worse-off than when they went in. Some never came back.

Things were going along pretty much as planned. We even thought about traveling. Then one day, my usually stoic husband complained about pains in his lower back and feeling more tired than usual. He started popping aspirin like it was candy, but it couldn't stop the bouts of pain which plagued him, along with the headaches, nausea and loss of appetite. He got a bad rash on both his legs and his skin started itching. One day when it was already ninety degrees in the house, he said that he was freezing. That's when I told him that we were going to the doctor's office."

"What was that doctor's name, Mrs. Palmer?" asked Detective Patterson.

"Uh, Dr. Harold King, Primary Care. He ran a solo-practice, with support from a receptionist and two full-time nurses. We rarely went to see him before that. Besides he didn't spend a lot of time with you unless he found a real problem. This time things were different. He spent almost a full hour with us, ordered a battery of tests and lab work, and personally set a follow-up appointment date for the following week. When we got there, the somber look on his face confirmed my worst fears. Thomas had end-stage renal disease. The doctor explained that it was a progressive disease with symptoms possibly dismissed as due to something else. His stoic attitude had not helped. Whatever the reason, his kidneys were failing.

Dr. King referred us to a specialist, a nephrologist, who said that Thomas would have to go on dialysis right away. Those words hit both of us like a bomb. I remember feeling numb. But, I'll never forget the look of desperation and hopelessness in my husband's eyes. I wanted to fix it, make it go away. But it was not up to me. What I could do was stay positive and be there to help him. I started by trying to find the right words. I thought that saying them enough would make them come true. I remember what I told him, 'We can beat this, sweetheart. Just do what the doctor's say and everything will be fine.' But, it was a losing battle.

The dialysis process was rough, to say the least. I could tell that it was wearing him down. Then one day on the way home he looked at me and sighed, 'I know that you are standing by me and I'm giving it the best that I've got. But, we both know where I'm going.'

He already had a bad heart. That was diagnosed while he was in the Army and the dialysis process made it worse. His nephrologist referred us to a cardiologist with a military background overseas somewhere who was now in civilian practice in Houston. A referral was made and an appointment date was set."

"What was the name of the cardiologist?" asked Detective Patterson.

"Uh, Ed, Dr. Edward Fernandez, that's it. There was nothing special about that first office visit. Oh wait, I just remembered something."

"What's that, Mrs. Palmer?"

"It was the way they looked at each other. It all happened so suddenly. When the doctor came into the room, I thought I saw him give Thomas a dirty *I got you now, sucka!* kind of look, like he was angry at him about something. Then seeing me in the room, he quickly plastered his face with a smile that was obviously fake. Thomas just sat there looking at him, his jaw clinched and the pupils of his black eyes so dilated that no white was visible. People have to have a reason for looking at each other like that, don't they? Other than that, everything proceeded just as you would expect. Dr. Fernandez prescribed some pills and a follow up appointment was set for the next month. At least that's what I thought."

"What do you mean?" asked Detective Riley.

"I found out that they had *history* with each other."

Chapter 13

Petey left the Army behind him with a spotless record and a position of sorts. Dr. Fernandez kept his promise and then some. Profits rolled-in, at least for a few weeks. Then, one day things fell apart. Parting on friendly terms, and with money in his wallet, Petey headed back to the States anxious for a reunion with his brother, Malik. He made a bee-line from the airport to the gym, expecting that Malik would be there working-out. George, one of the guys from the old crew, saw him come into the building and rushed over to greet him.

"Well, look what the cat dragged-in. Petey, where you been?" asked George.

"Doin a stent with Uncle Sam overseas. Where's Malik?"

"He comes in sometimes, but not today. Brother do I have some news for you. You remember *little Sheila*?"

"Yeah, what about her?"

"Right after you left town, Malik signed-on as her training partner. I guess he wanted to use what you taught him to help her win that competition she was training for. Between you and me, he really thought that she was his lady. Boy was he wrong about that! He missed one session, she met another guy and kicked your brother to the curb. That guy worked with her all right - they got married! Can you beat that?"

There were no words for what Petey was thinking. Malik was his little brother and he never wanted for any hurt to befall him. Somehow he failed him. Was he too hard on him? Was he too selfish? Now it was all water under the bridge. He was the oldest and it was up to him to salvage and fix what remained of their broken relationship. Malik was in terrible shape when he left for the Army. He was in physical and emotional pain. So, he would find his little brother, and build him back up the right way. He would start with this Sheila incident. Malik and Sheila grew up together. She belonged to Malik. How could she hurt him like that. Yes, she was married but he could do something about that. All he had to do was find this guy and make him, disappear.

"Hey, man, what was the name of the guy she married?"

George stood there, stroking his chin for a second before answering. "I think it was … Thomas. Yeah, Thomas Palmer. You remember him, don't you?"

Petey looked at him, his eyes wide and mouth open. "Did you say… Thomas Palmer?"

"Yeah, tall brown-skinned muscular brother with black eyes. I never saw anybody with eyes that black. Looked like some kind of gangster if you know what I mean. Turns out he was a home boy."

"What?"

"That's right. Grew up right here in the Projects with us. We all went to Wheatley High. Sure, I know you remember him. He was in our class but kept a low profile. He had to beef-up, being in the ROTC

78

program and all. He was a regular in here but trained by himself, usually around the time that Sheila worked-out. I remember a couple of the guys saying that he was trying to find-out information about her. He even asked me who that lady with the "champagne wishes and caviar dreams" was, but I didn't tell him anything. I was watching-out for Malik's interests, him being your brother and all. Man, he really watched her on the sly as she worked-out. Never tried to talk to her, back then. Word was that he joined the Army right after graduation. Very weird. Must have done well for himself to have Sheila interested in him. Heard they got a real nice brick house over in the Third Ward on Cleburne."

"Well ... if you see Malik, tell him I'm back and lookin for him."

"Will do," said George. Reaching in his pocket for something to write on, he quickly added, "Say, give me your cell number so we can get together." Petey wrote his number on the paper and gave it to George who promptly crumpled it up and put it in his pocket. George stood there, waving to Petey as he walked away. But Petey didn't notice. His mind was already miles away, planning his next move.

Chapter 14

The ashtray on the table was starting to overflow with butts and ashes. Detective Patterson reached for it and dumped the contents into the trash can. Taking another cigarette from his pack, he lit it, inhaling deeply before continuing with the interrogation. "Mrs. Palmer, you said that the doctor and your husband had history with each other. What did you mean by that?"

"They weren't strangers. They knew each other from the Army. Thomas was pretty quiet during the drive back home from the doctor's office. It wasn't long after we got home that someone called his cell phone. They didn't talk for long but the conversation was heated. He went into the bathroom and left the phone on the bed; so, I checked his messages. The person he was talking to also sent him a text message to meet him later that evening. It said he was anxious to talk about *old times*. I had just enough time to read that message and put his phone on the bed before he came back into the room. Thomas told me that he was going out and might be back late. It wasn't like him not to tell me where he was going, especially with his medical issues. Not wanting to upset him, I didn't ask questions. When he left I followed him and saw him go into a bar. I looked through the window and saw him sitting in a booth with that doctor, all buddy

buddy like. Given that office visit and that text message, how could that be? Something wasn't right. I got back home before he did. So the next day while he was away I hired a private detective... Jerry White."

Detective Patterson had been steadily taking notes. When he heard that name he looked up at Sheila, his eyes squinted and his brow furrowed. "You mean the guy we found on the floor at the cemetery, still alive and leaking blood?"

"Yes, one in the same. He's going to be ok, isn't he?" she asked, eyes filing with tears and bottom lip beginning to quiver.

"We don't know yet," said Detective Patterson. "I'll give the hospital a call after a while."

Her coffee was still steaming hot. Sheila took a sip, then continued her story. "After that Thomas found an excuse to go out no less than twice each week for those mysterious meetings. He always went to the same bar and always met with Edward, Dr. Fernandez. They didn't know that the bartender was an informant for Jerry. According to the bartender, one night Edward was really pumping my husband for information about something having to do with money. Thomas said he didn't know anything about it, but Edward wouldn't let it go. He jumped down Thomas' throat and Thomas told him where he could get off. Security came over and told them to take it outside. I heard that Thomas stormed out leaving Edward all by himself, angrily nursing what was left of his drink. Jerry told me all about it. Whatever was said really upset Thomas. He came home complaining about how badly he was feeling and saying that I didn't have to worry about him going out for any more meetings. He was hurting so bad that I took him to the hospital. Unfortunately, it turned out that Dr. Fernandez was also the cardiologist in residence at the hospital. They decided to keep him for observation and immediately put him on a morphine drip. I was sitting by his bed and will never forget the look on his face when he walked into Thomas' room.

Thomas was groggy from the medication, but he said, 'Dr. Fernandez?' The doctor snapped back, '*Mr. Palmer,* so, what's going on?' Thomas replied sharply, 'You tell me, *doctor*.'

"Well sometimes that doctor used technical lingo that, with his strong accent, made it hard to understand what he was saying. But after a while that problem worked itself out. It was their tone of voice that told me there was something awful between them; but, I was clueless as to what it was and Thomas didn't volunteer to fill me in. I did know that there was something about him I didn't like. He just gave-off a bad vibe. He had one of those funny looking mouths."

Detective Patterson laughed quietly, "Could you be more specific about his mouth?"

"His lower jaw jutted out beyond his upper lip and his teeth were all messed-up."

Taking a drag of his cigarette he said, "Ok, I get the picture. Please continue."

"The doctor said that Thomas needed an exploratory something or other procedure, just routine, nothing to worry about. It sounded so reasonable as he explained it, given the circumstances. But, I later learned that the *do no harm* oath he took was the last thing on his mind. In fact, he was purposely going to botch the procedure and disguise it to look like an unfortunate accident. He was planning to kill my husband."

Trying her best to read her partner, Detective Riley watched his eyes. Detective Patterson had the kind of faraway look so characteristic of someone lost in deep thought. Actually he was letting Sheilas' words paint a picture in his mind of what happened in that hospital room. What kind of a scum-bag, let alone a doctor, could possibly think that he could get away with a crime like that. He scanned Sheila's face, noticing how her eyes shifted focus from left to right when recalling the incident. His scan was being done for a reason which suddenly hit his partner. He was watching the pupils of Sheila's eyes, noting in what direction they shifted. It was some kind of ... honesty screening. What Detective Riley didn't realize was that her partner was also watching her. The look of recognition on her face told him that his partner passed his test with flying colors.

Chapter 15

Sheila was not one to run from anything. She always fought for what others told her she should be like, found a way to become it, no matter how she felt or how difficult the journey might be. This time things were different. This time the stakes were as high as they could get. This time she was running her own race. She was neither a raving lunatic to be sent to the funny farm or a cold blooded killer bound for the electric chair. There was only one truth about what really happened in that cemetery. That she would keep all to herself. She would tell the detectives only what they could understand and believe.

Memories of her life with Thomas flashed through her mind like images across a screen in a movie theatre. Every trial and tribulation encountered was now seared deep within her soul. In retrospect, she realized that she had to cross burning sands to get to a place of light and love. With hindsight, the journey would have been a lot easier.

His pack of cigarettes almost empty, Detective Patterson looked at Sheila and said, "Mrs. Palmer, would you like to take a break? You've been in here so long. It's ok if you want to."

"No, I need to get through this if it's alright with you?"

"Ok," he said. *I'll hold-out as long as I can. The machine is just down the hallway if I really get ... needy.*

You were just about to tell us what happened, starting with the procedure."

"Yes, well the life we had suddenly filled with doom and gloom. They prepped Thomas, then took him from the room. I stood in the doorway as they wheeled him out, and made some kind of flip comment like, 'See ya later alligator.' I remember him looking up at me, smiling bravely, saying, 'After a while, crocodile.' I remember going to the nurses station several times to find out what was happening. At first, they said not to worry, it was always like that. Then their voices became hushed and they avoided answering my questions. What should have taken only a few minutes turned into several hours. I was still waiting in the room when I heard the sounds of muffled voices in the hallway by the door. Dr. Fernandez walked in, accompanied by a nurse and a woman who identified herself as a hospital administrator. Something in my gut warned me that nothing good was coming from that meeting.

No one was smiling, which did everything but calm my growing anxiety. I said, 'What's going on? Where's my husband? Where's Thomas?' I was screaming and didn't care that I might be disturbing others.

The doctor's tone of voice was dry, patronizing, without compassion or pity. He said, 'Mrs. Palmer, calm yourself. I'm afraid I have some bad news. Sit down.'

I felt like I was just a task that he wanted to finish as quickly as possible. I said, 'Tell me.'

With a straight face and a measured tone, he said, 'Your husband died on the table.'

I blacked-out or something. The next thing I remember is lying on the floor with them standing around me, fanning me, and rubbing my arms and hands. I could hear them calling my name, but it took a long time before I could make out their words. I thought that I heard the nurse say something about seeing a blue mist or some kind of smoke hovering right over Thomas' body at the moment of death. But, I wouldn't swear to it.

Dr. Fernandez was coping the plea of the century. I could just make-out what he said because of his accent and because he was so nervous.

He said, 'I did what I thought was right, everything … indicated. How could I know he was allergic to that medication? It wasn't in his records. The hospital … should have done a better job at his pre-op appointment. It's not my fault … his heart gave out.' Then I heard a woman, probably the administrator tell him not to worry, that the record would reflect *the right chronology of events.'*

Detective Riley was silent. Then she said, "That was … unconscionable." It may just have been a coincidence that their eyes met, but the anger Detective Patterson saw there flamed his own feeling of righteous indignation at what happened in that hospital room. This was not the first time he had heard about this kind of thing happening. Too often evidence had been thrown out of court on the basis of a technicality leaving the cries of victims unavenged.

A lump was forming in Detective Riley's throat, growing larger as Sheila told her story. Her words brought back memories of what happened to her own younger brother, the only person that she had ever cared for in her life. He died at a young age during what was to have been a routine surgical procedure. She suspected that his doctor was at fault but the hospital covered it up and no lawyer would risk a tarnished track record by possibly losing the case. Her parents had always wanted him to become a policeman, just like their father. After his death, they groomed her to fulfill their dream for him. It was not her first choice of a profession, but it made her parents … happy. Her instincts kicking-in, she took a deep breath and felt the muscles in her throat relax. Her voice back to normal, she asked, "The hospital administrator didn't see any irregularities with what happened?" The silence that followed was deafening and all that was needed to answer her question.

"No. They let me see the body and contact a funeral home. That was all. I was numb but somehow got home. The only person I could think to call was Jerry. He's such a nice guy and I wanted him to know what happened. I was upset, but he calmed me down enough to hear what he had to tell me."

"What was that?" asked Detective Patterson.

"… that my husband's death was no accident."

Detective Patterson had been doodling on his paper. Hearing what Sheila said, he quickly looked up at her, eyebrows raised and eyes wide open. "So what you're saying is that this doctor, uh… Fernandez did something on purpose to kill your husband?"

"Yes. It seems that Thomas and Edward met overseas while they were in the Army. Edward came to America as a child from the Philippines. He attended medical school here and then enlisted in the Army as a doctor. The Army paid for his training to become a cardiologist. He spoke both English and Tagalog, and was sent to a base in the Philippines. That's where he met Thomas. They ran with the same fast crowd. They struck-up a relationship and soon discovered they had something besides the Army in common - a desire to make a lot of money, any way

87

possible and as quickly as possible. If a man wanted to run the risk, and had the resources, he could get rich quick by smuggling stolen cars back into the States. The more high-end, the better. Once cars were stateside, they were sold at auctions or stripped down for parts at chop shops. They stashed profits in off-shore bank accounts and gradually funneled money back into this country. No criminal mind could resist that kind of sweet deal. Jerry said there was another man in their circle, but he was still trying to find out who it was."

"You had no idea what was going on?" asked Detective Riley.

"Not a clue. Jerry said that according to his sources, Thomas cut the strings with those guys after he got out of the Army. Something happened about the money, so he called it quits and moved on with his life. This was the first time he had seen Dr. Fernandez since that happened."

"So the motive for killing your husband was … about money?"

"Most likely," said Sheila.

Something she said made him wonder if his friend had crossed the line with this suspect. There was no law against it, but it could become … problematic. Detective Patterson paused for a second before continuing. "You said that you hired Jerry White to do private detective work for you. What made you decide on him?"

Smiling, Sheila said, "That's easy. Remember that I said I followed Thomas to the bar and saw him talking with Edward. Something wasn't right and I didn't know what to do. Detective Patterson, do you watch "who-done-it" shows on television?"

"Not really," he replied, guessing he knew what she was about to say.

"Well, I do. I'm a big fan. Everyone knows to call a private detective when you want to uncover the truth, especially in a situation like this. That's just what you do. I looked in the Yellow Pages and liked his add. I called him at his office and we arranged to do everything by phone and mail. I hired him to do a background check on Thomas and Edward, find out what was going on. I didn't want to risk Thomas finding out. In fact, it was a while before I met him in person. Such a nice man."

"I just wondered. It was something you said a few minutes ago. Most of us know each other, being in the same line of work, you understand. I've known Jerry for a long time. He's a loner ... doesn't take to people easily. Seems like the two of you hit it off pretty well?"

Sheila picked-up on his not-so-subtle attempt to see if her relationship with Jerry was anything other than professional. It was, and it wouldn't take much for her to reveal it's true nature. It all started innocently enough, with him calling her to give updates about his progress on the job she was paying him to do. Then as the conversations became more frequent they began to connect at a deeper level. It was as if she had known him forever. Sheila was looking for something to replace the loss of intimacy in her life. She was the kind of person that Jerry, the loner, could unwind with. Her voice was soothing, and her words cheered him, blotting-out some of the ugliness inherent in his work. He was a good listener who accepted what she said unconditionally, exactly what she needed, given all of the drama around her. The tone of their conversations became friendly, and then more intimate with the passing of time, until the mere sound of his voice sent waves of desire pulsing throughout her body. Oh this detective was crafty. Well, it was none of his business. He would only get what she had already given him and nothing more. Her thoughts raced backwards in time to the night her husband died, the same night when she first met Jerry, face-to-face.

I was at the house, sobbing into one of Thomas' shirts, unable to comprehend what had just happened. Of all the people I could have called, Jerry's name was the one that came to mind. I called him at his office, knowing that it was the end of the work day but hoping he had time to hear what happened at the hospital. I had no idea that he would volunteer to come right over. But, he did, arriving shortly after the telephone call. Opening the door, I saw a man, not much older than me, tall, well built, casually dressed in a grey suit and brown loafers suitable for the humid Houston climate. Standing there with his jacket slung over one shoulder, he looked like someone you would see profiled in a top men's fashion magazine like GQ. The fact that I was only wearing a robe and slippers was really embarrassing, but the look in his sea foam green eyes told me that it didn't matter.

He walked into my living room, sat on the sofa next to me and listened patiently until I calmed down. Then without a word, he reached over and put his arms around me, pulling me close to him, gently kissing my tears away. The sweet spicy scent of his cologne was comforting, like hot chocolate on a cold winter's night. He said, 'We both want this, so hush ... just let it be.' I looked into his eyes and knew that everything said during our many telephone conversations was true. To my surprise, he took my hands in his and kissed them, ever so gently. I didn't object when he reached for me, loosening the belt until my robe fell to the floor. He leisurely began to undress, his clothes falling in a heap next to mine revealing his athletic build, well-defined six-pack abs, and obviously turned-on state. The two bracelets he wore on his right arm - one black with small beads and the other brown woven, stood out against his skin, the color of coffee, smooth as satin.

He left me, walked to the bathroom, and returned with two towels and a bottle of lotion which he placed on the floor in front of me. Going into the kitchen, he filled two large bowls with warm water, then returned to the living room, placing them on the floor close to me. Like the knights of long ago, he knelt before me as if I were his queen and gently removed my slippers. He guided my right foot into one of the bowls and moved the water over and around it like a gentle wave. His touch felt strangely, familiar.

After a while, he lifted my foot from the bowl, patted it dry, and wrapped it in one of the towels to keep it warm. The same care was taken with my left foot. Opening the bottle of lotion, he warmed some in his hands then massaged both feet, squeezing and stroking until I thought I would go mad. Then laying me back on the sofa, he gently caressed my breasts, squeezing the nipples until they stood firm and erect. 'Teach me how to love you,' he murmured. My hands on his, I began to glide them slowly across my body, guiding him to my pleasure spots as he lightly bit my lips, then thrust his tongue deep inside my mouth. What the hell was I doing? My husband's body barely cold and I was here like this with Jerry. For a second I swore that I smelled the woody musk scent of the cologne Thomas used to wear, hovering around me then gradually disappearing. But, how could that be? He was dead... and I was alive. When I needed comfort, he withheld it except to satisfy his own needs. Now it was too late. Now it was my turn. I needed to love and be loved by this man, so what the hell.

The hours passed, filled with gentle caresses and erotic sensations. Hidden from the world, our passion fell and rose. We came together as one, playing out a lover's scene from a story as ageless as time itself.

Lord knows she didn't want to get Jerry into trouble. Steeling herself and with as little emotion as possible, Sheila looked at Detective Patterson and said, "Yes, calling Jerry was one of the best things I ever did."

Chapter 16

Petey didn't have a pot to piss in or a window to throw it out of. Nevertheless, he found a decent looking Section 8 house for rent on Emancipation Avenue that was not far from his old neighborhood. He was lying on his bed one night when George called.

"Hey man, this is George. Remember me from the gym? You asked me about Sheila and I told you she got married to that guy ... Thomas. Did you hear the news?"

"Yeah I remember you. Did you find-out their address? I'd like to ... congratulate her."

"Don't rush ... I heard he died just this week."

The news was coming at him faster than he could process it. Petey sat-up and took a deep breath before continuing. "Wait a minute, he's dead?"

"Yeah," said George. "Something was wrong with his kidneys and he had a heart attack. So sad. Say, his heart doctor was also in the Army. You might have known him, a ... Dr. Edward Fernandez, had an office over on Dowling Street not far from the University. If you still want her number, I can get it from some of the guys at the gym. Let me know. Got to run. Catch you later."

It wasn't long before Petey was on his cell phone.

"Hey Edward..."

"Who's this ... Petey? Do you know what time it is? "

"Oh yeah. Say, I got news you want to hear."

"It better be good, waking me up. Go ahead."

"You told me that you were lookin for Thomas Palmer?"

"Yeah, so what?"

"I found him. He's dead."

" Is that why you called me? Fool… I know he's dead." Pausing, he said, "I … uh, where are you calling me from?"

"Oh, I'm back in Houston. Got a place over on Emancipation Avenue. Where are you?"

"Never mind. All you need is my cell number. Listen, we need to talk, but in person. I know a place, Ebb Tide… a Jazz Supper Club not too far from you. Can you meet me tomorrow night, say around nine?"

"I'll be there," said Petey. *I'll sure enough be there.*

***

Detective Patterson expected by now his wife had figured-out that he wasn't going to make it home in time for dinner. He could imagine her, sighing, taking the plate from the table and putting it in the refrigerator. But he wasn't about to rush this suspect. He would let her talk, reveal her story at her own pace, even if it took all night. Sooner or later- the truth would be told. Trying not to let Sheila catch him gazing wistfully at the clock, he said, "Sorry to hear that things went like that at the hospital. Do you know if your husband had any other enemies?"

"Not that I know of."

"Ok, what happened next?"

"Well, Thomas was dead. But, Jerry was still on the job. There was more that he needed to tell me and since he would be working late that night we decided to continue the conversation over dinner at a place not far from my house. He didn't want me to drive over there by myself so he volunteered to pick me up. A working-dinner, you understand."

Wondering why she would think otherwise, Detective Patterson said, "Of course, Mrs. Palmer."

Not wanting to get Jerry into trouble, Sheila hoped that the faint smile crossing her face had gone unnoticed. But, she couldn't hold it back. She remembered how Jerry looked the next morning when he walked into her bedroom.

He was holding a cup of freshly brewed coffee. 'Morning, baby. I have to go into work today. But, let's do something fun tonight. How about I take you out to dinner. There's a place not too far from here, not real fancy but I think you'll like it. It suits your ... dark and stormy personality.' Startled by his comment, I asked him why he thought my personality was dark and stormy. Jerry looked at me, his brow furrowed and said that it just came to mind. I asked him if us being seen together would cause problems for him. He told me not to worry about it. Besides, a night out on the town might be just what the doctor ordered.

"What was the name of the place?" asked Detective Riley.

"Ebb Tide."

With a wistful look in her eye and a sigh, Detective Riley replied, "Yes, I've heard of it. "

"I wanted to look nice so I went shopping in my closet. I'll bet you know what that's like, Detective Riley."

"Well, honestly I don't get much of an opportunity to do that, Mrs. Palmer. We have a dress policy."

"I picked something that was sure to pass any dress code - an off-the-shoulder, form-fitted dress that was kinda sparkly, with a matching shawl and sling-back pumps."

"That was a wise move." Then Detective Riley added, "They say the atmosphere is very nice. And, those places usually do have dress codes." *That's it. Connect with her. Gain her confidence*, thought Detective Patterson.

"I'll say. Jerry didn't tell me that it was a jazz supper club. But he was right. Getting out of my house worked wonders. Walking in there was like being on another planet. It was a little sleazy but it didn't matter because I couldn't have been more pleased with his choice.

It was around eight thirty and already dark when Jerry knocked on my door. His car was parked in my driveway. As we walked toward it, I could see that it was a sports car, silver in color and larger than the one that Thomas drove. With a proud grin on his face, he told me it was a Chevrolet Camaro, American made. The deal he made on it, while more than he could comfortably afford at the time, made it a good investment for the future. The leather Recaro seats, cool against my skin, hugged me like I was in a cocoon. He offered to let me drive it sometimes, just to get the feel of the automatic transmission. We raced down MacGregor Way, sunroof open, and Pharrell Williams singing "Like a room without a roof." Suddenly I felt ... complete. It was wonderful!

We walked into the place and were hit with a riot of smells - fish, smoke, and perfume. Our table wasn't quite ready, which gave us time to check-out the menu. The restaurant was well-known for spicy, hot gumbo. So, that's what we ordered - two bowls of steaming hot Texas seafood gumbo, with red beans and rice on the side and peach cobbler. Our decision made, we had plenty of time to sit at the bar, relax and appreciate how nicely the dimly-lit, rich atmosphere transformed the huge main dining area into a casual setting. There was also a smaller outdoor patio packed with bistro-like tables and an adjoining dance floor, well-worn, just large enough to accommodate a three-piece combo and a few bodies, swaying and sweating to the beat. Jerry made me laugh when he said that the dancers were "high steppin and low bending." There was a lot of activity and noise around us, but it wasn't loud enough to block out the sound of two voices, both male and very familiar. They were a few seats away but we easily overheard their conversation. I bet you can't guess who they were?"

The detectives looked at each other. Shrugging his shoulders, Detective Patterson said, "Is that a trick question, Mrs. Palmer?"

"Petey and Dr. Fernandez. Jerry had his back to them and I turned my head so that they couldn't see my face. I didn't catch much of what they said, but I heard Dr. Fernandez, Edward, mention Thomas' name. They were still sitting at the bar when the waitress came over to tell us that our table was ready. I'm sure that they didn't see us, and luckily our table was at the other end of the dining area."

"We got his last name," said Detective Patterson. "Just call him Edward. So what happened then?"

"We tried to not let that spoil our night out. The waitress was one of those flirty pretty young things, short afro crowning a flawless almond-shaped face, cat-like eyes, inch-long false eyelashes and an hour-glass figure. I'll have to give it to Jerry- aside from a few casual

97

glances while ordering, his gaze was riveted on me like super glue."

A look of satisfaction crept across Detective Patterson's face. *Now I've got you*, he thought. "Was that important to you, Mrs. Palmer?"

"Wouldn't it be important to any woman in the company of a handsome man, Detective Patterson?"

"Touche', Mrs. Palmer, touche'. So what happened next?"

"Jerry asked me if I remembered him saying that there was another man working with Edward and Thomas. What we overheard at the bar left no doubt that Petey was that man."

***

Petey was in seventh heaven. A man with his limited resources couldn't afford anything on the menu of a swell place like Ebb Tide, including the bar drinks. But as an invited guest? Now that was different. He would make the most of the opportunity - kiss-up to the doctor and have a good time while doing it.

"Say Edward, this is a nice place. Since you invited me, I'll assume you're footing the bill?"

Edward glared at Petey and with a sarcastic smile said, "Uh ... well ... alright, but only drinks. What'll you have?"

Without hesitation, Petey said, "Whisky, straight-up for me."

"Bartender, I'll have a vodka and my friend will have a ... small whisky, straight-up. So, like I was saying on the phone, I know that Thomas Palmer is dead. I killed him."

"You did what?" yelled Petey, momentarily forgetting how crowded together people were.

Edward snapped back, "Keep your voice down."

Noticeably on-edge about possibly being overheard, he answered in a tone that was just above a whisper. "I said, I killed him. Too bad that it had to be that way. We knew each other from overseas. We had such a sweet deal going with those cars. I figured something was wrong when he stopped returning my calls." Taking a sip of his drink, Edward continued, "I started getting complaints from customers that he wasn't showing-up to deliver goods. Some even threatened me - return their money, or else. Something told me to check the bank-accounts and wouldn't you know it - a lot of money was missing. So, I put two and two together. It was as plain as the nose on your face. That cheating bastard was stealing from me, his own partner. Naturally, I had to close-up shop. Remember? I didn't want to do that to you, Petey. We got along just fine, you and me. But that Thomas ..."

Edward took another sip. Talking about Thomas brought back all the anger he felt towards him along with the feeling of satisfaction he got from seeing his lifeless body lying on that hospital gurney. Stilling his thoughts, he said, " I kept my promise. I found him and made him pay for his *indiscretion*. Now, all that remains is to find-out where he stashed my ... the money."

Wanting nothing more than to be thick as thieves with Edward, Petey looked at him and said, "Man, you ... we ... really got screwed. I hear you. You gotta do what you gotta do. So, where do you think he stashed all that money?"

"I've been thinking about that. Sometimes the best place to hide something is in plain sight."

"Meaning?"

"Suppose a man had a wife and that wife had a bank account that he had access to, you know, both their names on it."

"Uh, huh… oh, I see. You think he stashed the money in her account?"

Edward looked at Petey, amazed that anyone could possibly be that dense. Trying his best to keep from laughing out loud, he said, "Petey, you're a genius."

"But, wouldn't she have noticed?"

"Possibly, unless he duped her into believing that he was better at handling the finances. I knew Thomas. He liked to be in control. My bet is that was just what he did."

"So, what's the next move, boss?"

"Boss … I like the sound of that. Well, this Sheila, she's a widow now. We've got to find a way to move-in on her and get access to that money. Say, Petey, didn't you tell me you were lookin-out for your younger brother, Malik?"

"Yeah, what about him?"

"He and Sheila were about the same age. Maybe they knew each other? Maybe you'd like to kill two birds with one stone?"

"Oh yeah, I get it. I get it!"

"Thought you eventually would, my man."

Chapter 17

❝Jerry and I sat at our table, eating dinner, listening to the music and watching people dance. We suspected that Edward was to blame for Thomas' death. But we needed proof. Petey was mixed-up in it, but how? And, why was Edward riding Thomas that night in the bar about money? Was that why they split-up? We sat there almost until the place closed reviewing everything. However, first things first. My husband was dead and the mortuary was waiting for me to make the final arrangements. At Jerry's suggestion, I got an autopsy which confirmed the cause of death as a heart attack. A simple service was held at the mortuary chapel attended by myself, a few close friends, and a full honor guard befitting his military status. I don't know why but I decided to be present at the cremation.❞

Detective Patterson looked at Sheila and said quietly, "I don't know if I would have had the courage to do that."

"No, I will never do it again - knowing what it's like, what I saw, what I *smelled*. The mortuary even had me sign a statement that I wouldn't sue them if I developed … emotional issues after seeing it. I thought it would be easy to forget, but I still have nightmares. I can still see his body on that cremation slab, skin waxy like a department store mannequin. I can still smell the formaldehyde, feel the sudden rush of hot air on my face as I pushed the green button that opened the oven door, see his body sliding into the furnace."

Both detectives were becoming more understanding of the pressure Sheila had been under. Being at a loss for words, everyone remained silent for what seemed like an eternity. Sheila was the first to speak. "Since I had already purchased an urn and niche in the columbarium at the cemetery, and because the cremation was so stressful, I had them place the ashes and notify me when everything was done."

Seeing the questioning look on his partner's face, Detective Patterson quickly said, "Uh, just for clarification ... cremation ashes are placed in urns, urns are placed in niches - holding spaces, in columbarium's - buildings housing the niches." Detective Riley flashed a smile, grateful for the explanation.

"All that remained was for me to drive to the cemetery and confirm that everything was ... satisfactory. Jerry had never seen a columbarium before and offered to go with me, but I thought it best that I go alone." Sheila hesitated for a second, then added, "Uh, this is going to sound - strange, but I swear, it's the truth. The night before I was to go to the cemetery, I was getting ready for bed when suddenly, only for a second, I had a feeling that something ... strange, was going to happen to me. Then when I went to bed I had - that dream, the one I told you about when you brought me in for questioning. The next day, it all came true just as in my dream - the drive, the tall gates, the bad weather, the flagpole, the buildings, the condition of the graves, everything!"

Once again, the room fell silent. Detective Patterson looked at Sheila and said, "Mrs. Palmer, I ..."

Before he could finish, Sheila said, "What I feared most was waiting for me at the end of that path - walking into the columbarium, seeing the niche and the funeral urn with my husband's ashes. You see, the front side of each niche is made of glass and lift's up so you can get inside. You can actually look-in and see the urns and little keep-sakes. Anyway, the building only has one entrance door. You walk directly into the lobby and then see several corridors leading to where the niches are. Benches are in each corridor so you can sit and meditate. I found the corridor that I wanted, then saw the niche where Thomas' ashes were. As I stood there I swear I heard *his* voice, Thomas' deep voice, speaking to me. At first it was muffled, as if coming from some far-away place. Then, gradually it became so clear that it sounded like he was standing next to me."

Detective Patterson felt a chill run down his spine. Lasting only for a second, it reminded him of the way he felt as a young boy, sitting beside his grandfather on chilly Autumn nights while he told ghost stories. It didn't take a rocket scientist to figure-out what the next question should be. But who would ask it? Summoning his courage, he took a deep breath and jumped in with both feet. "What did he say?"

Sheila looked at him, repeating the words exactly as she heard them. "Be careful. What we have now is fragile. We have to take care of our team, guard it so it will endure. We have to get rid of anything that might work against us."

Caught off-guard and struggling to hold back tears, Sheila finally regained her composure. "The whole thing really shook me up. Fortunately there was a bench right there or I would have fallen on the floor. That's when I heard someone come into the lobby - a maintenance man or maybe the caretaker, dressed in a blue uniform and carrying a utility bucket. He was checking the niches, making sure the glass fronts were secure. You see, people put a lot of valuable trinkets in those niches.

He reminded me of an old western movie character, slightly bent-over, shuffling his feet so as to carefully place his steps without falling. I thought to myself, *Poor man, I wonder why he doesn't use a cane?* His salt and pepper kinky hair was packed-down to follow the shape of his head. Wrinkles criss-crossed his tanned skin making him look so ... ancient. Somehow I knew that he meant me no harm. He saw me and when I didn't attempt to leave, came over and sat beside me. He smelled of cigarettes but not strong enough for me to complain. He said, 'Hi, my name is Ron. I'm t...t-the caretaker here. Are you okay?' His voice was raspy, maybe due to COPD, but strangely comforting.

Still shaken from hearing *that* voice, I didn't answer right away. He would only think I was some kind of nut case. Ron looked at me, his bushy eyebrows slightly raised to reveal grey eyes discolored with cataracts. Apologizing for my silence, I explained that those were my husband's ashes and that everything was still a little raw. That was when my tears started flowing. I sensed that he felt sorry for me and wanted to comfort me but was also concerned that his actions might be misinterpreted. He looked around the corridor and not seeing anyone, reached in his pocket and pulled out a small pack of tissues. He said, 'May I offer you a t ..., offer you a t...t-tissue? I keep several in my pocket, just for t..., for t-times like t ... t-this, and it's clean.' I smiled and gratefully accepted his offer.

The next day I went back to the cemetery and wasn't surprised to see Ron heading my way. He wasn't alone. A woman walked beside him, holding his hand. Her hair was almost completely grey and her step was quicker than expected for a woman of her advanced age. He told me that he lived right there on the property in the small house next to the parking lot and that the woman was his wife, Janie, who turned out to be as charming as her husband. He knew where I was going and said that he would be back after walking his wife home. I watched them, hand in hand, until they disappeared among the headstones. There was something about Ron. His presence was so comforting that I was starting to think of him as a father figure. I could tell that he was a smart guy even though he sometimes had trouble saying what was on his mind.

I made my way over to the columbarium and sat on the bench in front of the niche. Hearing footsteps, I turned around and saw Ron moving towards me. But something was ... different about him. He stood more erect than before, his shoulders thrown back, striding like he didn't have a care in the world. He sat on the bench beside me - almost like he was in a deep trance, didn't say a word, just looked at me then turned away, staring into space, beads of sweat popping-up on his forehead. The color of his eyes - no longer grey, they had become jet black! His wrinkles softened with a fuller, smoother expression. But it was when he spoke that I almost passed out. I knew *that* voice. It was Thomas' voice alright but the words were coming from Ron's mouth. 'Sheila don't be frightened. It's me, your Thomas.'

I thought to myself, *Sheila, you have finally gone over the edge.* (That was exactly what both detectives were thinking.) *You saw his body go into the oven. You're wearing a locket that holds some of his ashes. Maybe this is just a - hallucination? Yes, that's it - just a vision; but, it seems so damn ... real.* I called-out to Ron, but he didn't respond. He seemed to be asleep but not asleep ... definitely trancelike. There was no vent or window nearby, but I felt a cool breeze lightly brush my cheek.

The voice continued, 'I'm no longer sick. There is no pain.' I looked around the corridor, wanting to believe that someone was playing a practical joke on me. Determined to show that I wasn't going to be taken in that easily, I stood up, put my hands on my hips, and said, 'If this is real, then I should be able to see you.' Why did I say that? A light came from the niche, dim at first, then so bright that I had to turn away. When I looked back, I saw ... something that looked like Thomas. Yes, it *was* Thomas or what he had become. Bathed in a blue light, he stood there, smiling at me, looking as he did the first night that we met. I could even smell the woody musk scent of his cologne. Still refusing to believe, I reached-out to touch him and my fingers went right through his ... arm. He touched me, sending needle pricking sensations in my arm from my shoulder to my fingertips. He said, 'I have something important to tell you. The scales of life are sometimes unbalanced ... you must set them straight ... my death was no accident... get the proof ... watch your back ... our team will endure.' Then the blue light and everything within it began to fade until there was ... nothing.

I just sat there trying to understand what happened. Still slightly disoriented, Ron gradually became more alert and like his old self. He started talking to me as if nothing had happened, inviting me to supper that

Saturday around five o'clock because that was when he got off work. He said that it wouldn't be fancy, just a few of Janies' special dishes. I thanked him and asked if I could bring someone with me."

Stunned by what he just heard, Detective Patterson looked at Sheila. The only thing he could think of to say was, "What caused you to want to take someone with you to their home?"

"I liked them but they lived on the cemetery grounds and the thought of being there after dark was a little ... unsettling."

Detective Patterson's nose was twitching again. Somehow he knew the answer before even asking the question. "So, who went with you?"

"Jerry, I mean Mr. White."

Chapter 18

The male voice on the other end of the line gloated with sarcasm. "Hey Sheila, I bet you can't guess who this is?"

"No ... "

"It's me, Malik. Now come on baby, it hasn't been that long. Anyhow, I called because I heard what happened to uh ... your husband, Thomas."

"Yes... how did you get this number?"

"Oh, somebody gave it to me. *I got your address, too.* Listen, now that he's out of the picture, maybe we can get back together?"

"Malik, we were *never* together."

"Ah, don't be like that. Besides, I have some ... information that I'm sure you'll be interested in."

" ... about what?"

"Can't say over the phone. I'll come over tonight and we'll talk about it."

"Well ... my place is a mess. I'll meet you at, uh, Ebb Tide. It's a small jazz supper club not far from where I am."

"Yeah, I know the place. So you're inviting me to dinner?"

"No, I'm not! I'll meet you at the bar. You can pick up your own tab. I'll be there about nine."

"Okay, see ya."

***

Detective Patterson sighed. Another bottom-dollar bet was in the making. *It's not a crime to go out with Jerry. But you have no way of knowing that. Even so, when will you have the courage to be honest about your relationship.*

"What were you and Mr. White, let's just call him … Jerry, planning to do?"

"Well, as soon as Malik hung up, I called … Jerry and told him about the conversation with Malik. I didn't want to hold back on anything, because he was working for me, what with all the new stuff turning-up. He told me to go ahead with the meeting at Ebb Tide. He didn't tell me that he would also be there, but I kinda figured he would be somewhere in the place. He just didn't seem like the kind of guy who would let me walk in there by myself. I might not see him, but something told me that he would be there incognito, watching and listening.

"Sounds reasonable," said Detective Patterson. "He's not the kind of man who would let you go through that alone. What time did you get there?"

"… around eight forty-five. The place was beginning to get crowded but several bar stools were still empty. Jerry was already there, so I claimed the stool next to him and sat there waiting for Malik to come in." A faint smile crossed Sheila's face.

Detective Patterson caught her expression. "Something funny?"

"No … well yes. It's just that Jerry and I were right next to each other and Malik never made the connection. Anyway, it was about nine when Malik arrived, strutting across the room towards me just like his brother would

109

have done. The bottom line was that he tried to blackmail me - marry him or he would make my life miserable, maybe worse.

***

"What? No hugs and kisses for your old man?"

"Malik, tell me what you have to say so I can get out of here. It's been a very long day."

"Hold your horses, sweetie. What are you drinking?"

"I've got mine. Don't worry about it."

"Oh, ok. Well since you want to be that way, I won't beat around the bush. I'm gonna tell you a ... story about your darling husband, about what he was *really* into. It seems that he was hangin with some rough characters, got involved with some shady deals, and disappeared with a lot of cash leaving his partners high and dry. I hear those guys are still tryin to track that money down, if you know what I mean. And, now that he's ... no longer with us, guess who their eyes are on. Now, maybe I could find those guys and give them your number. By the way, I'll bet you didn't know that he was a regular at the gym and that he had the hots for you for a long time before the night you ... kicked me to the curb for no good reason. At least, that's what I heard."

Sheila took a sip of her drink. "How did you get this information?"

Malik grinned, "Now, wouldn't you love to know that. It's enough that I did."

"Well, talk is cheap. What do you want me to do about it?"

"Here's the deal. I can sing like a canary, shut-up like a clam, or … point them in another direction … it's up to you."

"And what do you want in return?"

"If I keep quiet? Not much … a small token of your gratitude. You're a free woman now. Marry me."

Just then the man sitting next to Malik bumped into him, spilling his drink all over his shirt sleeve in the process. His hooded eyes wide in indignation, Malik grabbed a paper napkin as he yelled, "Look out, you spilled your drink all over me." The smile on Sheila's face turned into a snicker as she watched him with satisfaction, knowing that the dark colored liquor had already stained the fabric beyond repair. Eyes half-closed and with a blank stare on his face, Jerry replied, "Sorry, must have had too much to drink. Bartender, this guy's next drink is … on me."

"Well, what's it gonna be?" growled Malik.

"I'll think about it. Give me some time. I have your number."

Not bothering to look back at Sheila, Malik got up and walked toward the door. "Don't take too long. I better get home and work on these stains."

"Yes," said Sheila. "You do that."

Chapter 19

Detective Riley watched her partner as he worked the investigation. There was much she could learn from him. He certainly lived up to his reputation. Seasoned and smooth, he knew when to back off and when to charge ahead. More importantly, he knew how to read the suspect's tell to catch lies. Not understanding the intricacies of how that worked was what got her reassigned to his unit. Her little treasure book discovered, she was unable to keep-up her front when questioned by her previous supervisor. Caught in a lie, was it a slip of the tongue or did she shift her eyes the wrong way? Yes, she was catching-on quickly.

"So Malik had something on Thomas," said Detective Patterson. "What was your next move?"

"Both of us were hungry and we also wanted to talk about what just happened, but couldn't take a chance that Malik might come back and see us together in the restaurant. So, we did something that no one would ever expect us to do - we went to my house. Jerry volunteered to cook dinner providing that I supplied the pots and pans." Sheila thought to herself, *they don't need to hear the intimate details. Some things are private, not meant to be shared with others.* Then she added, "The only thing we didn't count on was that Malik would change his plans about going home to clean-up. It turns out that he was lurking in the parking lot, waiting for me to come out, planning to follow me. I can just imagine what he thought when he saw me get into the car with Jerry."

***

Jerry was the first one to leave the club. Sheila waited for a few minutes, then made her exit to the parking lot where his car was parked in a partially secluded spot. Neither of them noticed the black Mustang pulling-out behind them only a few car-lengths away.

Stopping at a grocery store on the way, Jerry suggested that she sit in the car while he went in to do the shopping. He soon returned with a cart full of groceries which made her wonder just how many people he intended to cook for.

To be on the safe side, Jerry circled the block a couple of times before pulling into her driveway.

"I'll bring the groceries in," said Jerry.

The house was dark, so Sheila opened the front door and turned on the light in the living room but not on the front porch, just in case Malik was lurking out there.

"I'm going to pamper you tonight," he said. "Just go in and get … comfortable."

Realizing how tired she was, Sheila gladly accepted his offer. Once in the bedroom she started rummaging through her closet. Hoping for a repeat of their last encounter she didn't want to put on anything that was too … confining. She could hear Jerry moving about the kitchen, taking things out of the bags and even washing the few dishes she left in the sink. Satisfied with her choice of outfit, she headed for the kitchen and was totally unprepared for what awaited her. Jerry had not only cleared her kitchen table of the usual clutter stored on it, but transformed it to look like one you would find at the club they just left, complete with a new table cloth, long stemmed red roses, and her good china and place settings.

"How would you like your steak cooked - medium rare or well-done? Oh yeah, we also have a tossed green salad and baked potatoes with all the toppings."

Staring in amazement, she said, "Exactly how long was I in that bedroom?"

"Long enough," said Jerry, an impish grin lighting up his face.

"Well-done, please."

"Your wish is my command."

"What's the occasion?"

"Does there have to be a special occasion for me to treat you like the queen you are? Besides, I love to cook. When I was growing-up, my mother and father were always in the kitchen when they weren't working. I learned a lot from them. I was the oldest of three brothers and one sister. It was my job to look-out after them while my parents were at work. That included cooking dinner."

"That's right, I forgot that we both grew-up right here in Houston," said Sheila.

"Yeah, we lived in Third Ward on Ruth Street. I graduated from Jack Yates High then got my Bachelor's Degree from Prairie View A & M University in Criminal Justice. I'm in the graduate program now and almost finished. In the meantime, I started my own business. As soon as I get my doctorate the world will be my oyster. Ok, steaks are ready."

Seated at the table, Jerry spread a napkin across Sheila's lap. Then he filled both plates with food that could compete with that served in the best restaurants in town.

"Jerry, this is delicious."

"I'm glad you like it. I want you to keep your great figure, but I also hope eating like this will become a … habit for us. Anyway, let's talk shop for a few minutes. Malik is obviously getting direction from someone … smarter than he is. It's most likely his brother, Petey. And that doctor, Fernandez, has his footprints all over everything. Doctors keep records on patients. I'll bet he still has Thomas' file in his office. Those case notes - that's the proof about what really happened during that procedure. But, there's one catch. Obviously he won't give me permission to rifle through his file cabinets. I could break into his office, but that's a crime as well as a violation of our code of ethics. I've got to keep my record clean or I could lose my license, business and go to jail."

Without hesitation, Sheila said, "So, I'll do it."

"Now wait a minute. Stop and think about what you're saying. Do you realize the risk you'll be taking? What if he discovers you in there? He's the criminal, but doing that would make it too easy for you to become a victim of the criminal justice system. No, I'll think of another way."

Realizing that his concern for her welfare was heartfelt, Sheila said, "Jerry, this is something I feel I have to do. Do you remember that message I got from Thomas … you must set them straight … my death was no accident … get the proof. I think this is what he meant."

"No, that's not going to happen. There's got to be another way. Sheila, promise me that you won't do anything like that."

"Ok, ok, forget it." Taking another bite of her steak, she said, "We'll handle it another way."

"Good." Lacking the professional experience possessed by his friend, Detective Patterson, Jerry was not as knowledgeable about how to read a person's tell. Therefore, he had no idea that Sheila's promise amounted to no more than a pinkie swear.

Sheila rose and began stacking the dishes neatly in the sink. *As a matter of fact, it can go off this weekend.*

"By the way, the caretaker at the cemetery, Ron, invited me to supper at his home on Saturday. He and his wife, Janie are so nice. *That doctor's office is not that far from here. I can get that file before we go, get back here in time to go to dinner, then stash it in the niche during dinner. That's the one place where it will be safe until we need it. It won't take long and I can always think of some excuse to get away from dinner to do the job.* Gazing at Jerry with adoration and love, she added, " I already asked Ron if I could bring someone ... special with me. Do you mind?"

Jerry studied Sheila's face in a way that he had never done with any other woman. At that moment he was thankful that she had dropped the subject of a break-in. Before long he would have agreed to anything she said, right or wrong, lost as he was in the spell cast by her bewitching hazel eyes and seductive lips.

"Well, I'd love to meet them. Let's continue our conversation over .... desert .... in the bedroom. The dishes can wait."

Chapter 20

The first thing that Malik did when he got home was to call his big brother, Petey.

"Petey, this is Malik. I just saw Sheila."

"And …?"

"She wanted to know how I got her number. Of course I didn't tell her that George from the gym gave it to you or that you gave it to me."

"That was really smart," said Petey, all the time thinking *this conversation is too important. I'll have to dumb it down so genius can get it right.* "So, what happened?"

"Oh, I impressed her with my charms."

"Malik …"

"Just kidding. I told her that the price for my keeping quiet about Thomas was that she had to marry me."

"What did she say?"

"That she wanted to think about it and would call me. I told her not to take too long."

"Yeah, marry her, put your name on her bank accounts, then play with her - kick *her* to the curb, just like she did to you. I know that's where Thomas stashed all that money. Petey thought to himself, *a two-way split is better than a three-way split. There's got to be a way to cut Edward out of the mix.* Then you and me, well it's good times for us, little brother."

"I thought that she would be pretty lonely by now, what with Thomas out of the way. But I don't know. I think she might already be seeing someone."

"What makes you think that?" asked Petey.

"Well, some fool bumped into me at the bar and spilled his drink all over my shirt. I told her that I was going home to clean-up. "

"So ..."

"That's what I told her, but I really went out into the parking lot and waited for her to leave. Something bothered me about how that incident went down and I wanted to check-out my hunch. Sure enough, within a few minutes that same man walked out and got into a car. Then Sheila walked out and got into the car with him."

"Oh yeah? What did he look like?"

"It was dark, but he was kinda tall, real nice dresser, and had ... light-color green eyes, I think. I followed them. They stopped at a store, then drove to her house. I knew it was her house by the address you gave me. I parked across the street and waited for a long time but he never came-out. Finally it got so late that I went home."

"That's interesting ... very interesting. You know, it's good to have a back-up plan, just in case. So if she won't ... cooperate, then ... well, let's just say, there's always Plan B. Remember, the money is the prize. There are a lot of ... fish in the sea. Anyway, keep tailing them. I want to know how much time she actually spends with him and where he goes when he leaves her. And, Malik, keep a low profile."

"Will do."

***

Eager to stay in his good graces, Petey hung up the phone and called Edward.

"Edward, this is Petey. Remember what we talked about?"

"So, what's the good word?"

"Just talked with my little brother, Malik. He met with Sheila tonight and told her what she needed to do to keep him quiet. She's open to discussing it but, well ... there's more. I'll tell you later."

"Good job, my man ... good job. Keep me in the loop."

Chapter 21

Malik couldn't get Sheila out of his head. He never loved her - but, he would possess her. It was his destiny. She was his toy, his property, *his* lady. This time he would not be denied. Who did she think she was? Petey was right. For the next three nights he parked his car just far enough away so he could keep tabs on the going-ons at her house. Each night he saw the same silver colored Chevrolet Camaro pull into her driveway and leave just before the crack of dawn. Each time he saw the silhouette of a man exit the car and move discretely along the path to her front door. Each time the door opened, he saw the faint outline of her body, draped in something flimsy and seductive. What her naked body must look like, every curve, every angle! He imagined himself in that man's place until finally, he became that man, smelling her skin, discovering places to touch her to make her … wet, giving her the privilege of pleasuring his every desire, *his* every carnal urge.

His mind raced back to their childhood days in the Projects. Of course, she would say that as children he was the needy one who came to her to get what his family couldn't give him. But, that was a lie. She was the one who wanted him, needed him, *loved* him! Even as a child, she teased him, flaunting herself in front of him, starved for his attention and willing to do *whatever* it took to get it. She couldn't wait to get him to work with her in the gym because she knew that *his* knowledge was superior to hers. Did she really think there wouldn't be consequences for humiliating him in front of the guys? This new man was just an ... irritant. Now that Thomas was out of the way, he would move in and set things right. Who knows? If she treated him ... respectfully, maybe he would be nice to her - let her buy things, once he got his hands on all of that money. Of course in return she would have to show her appreciation, do *whatever* he demanded, even tolerate his need to be with other women. He would help her come to her senses. His relationship with Petey was important, but this thing with Sheila - now *that* was the trophy he wanted. One thing was for sure - he wasn't about to let anyone or anything take her from him. If the time ever came to dismiss her, if she became ... boring, then he would do it himself.

Chapter 22

The next few days came and went. Then on Saturday something different happened. Malik decided to start his surveillance earlier than usual. It was the rainy season in Houston and the day had been exceptionally stormy. Malik hated those dreary days because it was so hot and the humidity was higher than usual. He planned to spend as little time as possible sitting in his car, feeling miserable and rubbing condensation off the windows. Parking his Mustang across from Sheila's house, he had just started eating a chicken sandwich when he saw her get into her car and pull-out into the line of traffic still braving the terrible weather. Malik was so unprepared for what he saw that he almost dropped his sandwich in his lap while putting the key in the ignition. He followed her down rain-soaked streets, always keeping a few car lengths behind, until finally, she reached her destination. It was an office building over on Dowling Street, not far from the University.

***

Detective Patterson looked directly into Sheila's eyes. The interview had reached one of those pivotal moments and he wanted to make sure she understood the weight carried by the next words she would speak. He felt his jaw muscles tighten and his brow furrow. "Mrs. Palmer, were you planning to break into Dr. Fernandez's office and if you were, did you discuss those plans with Jerry?"

Sheila met his gaze without blinking and said, "I did what needed to be done. But I never told Jerry what I was planning to do. He was not involved."

Relieved by her answer, Detective Patterson relaxed as he exhaled a long breath. That was breaking and entering. His friend, Jerry, could lose the license and business he had worked so hard to get. "So you went to Edward's office, alone?"

"Yes, I did."

"What time did you arrive there?"

"… around three-thirty. It was Saturday and the weather was terrible, but I didn't want to get there too early. Some people work on the weekends. Edward's office was on the ground floor of the two story building. No one was there except for the maintenance crew cleaning the building. It would have been too obvious for me to use the front entrance, so I went in through a side door. I couldn't believe my luck - his office door was … unlocked! I guess the maintenance people left it that way while they took a break. I didn't know how much time I had, so I hurried through the reception area and went directly into his office. There was just enough light in there for me to go through his cabinet. Thomas' file was in there, just as I suspected! I didn't even stop to read it - just put it into a bag I had with me and made a quick exit. I'm pretty sure that no one saw me. As I was getting into my car, it dawned on me that I forgot to close the drawer. Hopefully the maintenance people noticed it and closed it before they left for the evening."

Sheila had no idea that Malik followed her and watched her enter the building. While she was in there, he spent the downtime sitting in the parking lot in his Mustang, trying to figure-out what could have possessed her to go out in that terrible weather, let alone to a building where the offices were closed for the weekend. And was that a bag she was carrying in her hand? Following her back to her house, he called Petey on his cell phone to let him know what was going on.

"Hey Petey, it's Malik."

" You caught me just as I was waking-up. This weather always makes me sleepy. What's up?"

" I'm following Sheila back to her house. I can't figure it out - she just drove across town in this rain to a building filled with closed offices, went in a side door, stayed there for a hot minute, then came back out carrying ... I don't know, something in a bag. What do you make of it?"

"Man, where was that building?"

"Down here on Dowling street, not too far from the University."

"Fool, that's Edwards office! Don't let her out of your sight. Ring me when you get to her house. I'm calling Edward now."

***

"Edward, this is Petey."

"Petey, it's my day off. What ..."

"Don't say a word, just listen. I talked to Malik. I think Sheila got into your office and took that file on Thomas.

124

Didn't it have your case notes in it about what happened during that procedure at the hospital?"

"Shit …. There was more than that in that file, *like the pin, account and routing numbers for all of those off-shore bank accounts.* Let me think for a minute. Ok, where is Malik now?"

"He's following her - looks like she's headed back to her house. I told him to call me when he got there."

"Ok … tell him to park across the street. I'm going to my office. Meet me there."

"Will do."

***

Detective Patterson could tell that both he and his partner were thinking the same thing. *This woman has a hell of a lot of brass.* "So when you found what you were looking for, what did you do?" he asked.

"I put the file in a bag and headed back to my house not knowing that Malik followed me. Anyhow, I made it just in time to meet Jerry. Then we drove to the … cemetery."

At last my tactics are going to pay-off. The waiting game is coming to an end. Detective Patterson pulled out another cigarette. Lighting it, he leaned toward Sheila and said, "I can't wait to hear what happened next."

Chapter 23

Sheila pulled into her driveway and went into her house. Malik parked across the street in his usual spot. The rain was starting to subside, but it was still windy enough to sway the clumps of moss back and forth that hung from the branches of the live oak trees lining the sidewalk.

Malik was just about to call Petey when the silver Camaro pulled into Sheila's driveway. A man wearing a raincoat and holding an umbrella made a mad dash for her front porch. Sheila answered the door, but instead of going back into the house, turned off the lights, walked onto the front porch, and closed the door behind her. And, she was carrying the same bag he saw her leave Edwards office with. He could just make-out the outline of the hem of her blue-jeans peeking out below her raincoat. They ran back to the driveway, got into the Camaro and pulled-out into traffic. This time the drive was longer, so he took his time calling Petey to let him know what was going on.

"Petey… Malik. Man, I can't believe it! I've been tailing them for about half an hour. Oh, wait, they're turning onto a gravel road. That's really going to mess-up my tires. Looks like some kind of … gate ahead … yeah, just passed through it… had angel figures all over it. Ok, there's a building ahead with a parking lot next to it. Looks like… no way, a church? I'll be able to get a better

126

look when I get closer. Right now I'm hangin-back so they won't see me. Ok, I don't believe it. It's still raining and windy, but they got out of the car, didn't go into that building but into a … house next to it. I'm pulling-up onto the parking lot. Dammit, it's starting to rain heavy again. Ok … now I can … wait a minute … this is a …cemetery! What the hell …"

"A … cemetery? Is that what you said? Malik?"

"Yeah …"

"Well I'll be a …," said Petey. "This couldn't be more convenient. Stay right where you are and keep out of sight. Listen carefully. Text me the exact directions. I'm calling Edward now. I'll pick him up from his office and then we're coming out there where you are. And Malik, remember what I said about having a Plan B?"

" Yeah …"

"I know we didn't … talk about the particulars but … this might be the night when somebody's gonna be pushing-up daisies."

"I don't understand …"

"That's alright, little brother, *that's alright* …"

Chapter 24

Sheila looked at the detectives. "We had dinner at Ron and Janie's home," she said. "I had it with me in a bag - the file I got from Edward's office. At some point, I slipped out and went to the columbarium. My plan was to get back before they missed me. But those guys - Petey, Malik, and Edward - saw me and followed me over there."

***

Ron was sitting in his favorite lounge chair. Rainy weather always made his arthritis flare-up, so he was happy to have the rest of the evening and Sunday to relax. Luckily their house was next to the parking lot, so it would be easy for Sheila to find it without him waiting outside in the pouring rain. He watched his wife, Janie, as she flitted around the small living room of their one-bedroom house. He loved teasing her about one thing or another and company coming was a perfect opportunity. He tried his best to sound annoyed, but something in his voice betrayed his true feelings.

"Janie, w...w-will you please sit down. T...t-this is not a model house. People live here. You're going t...t-to make yourself sick."

"Ron, don't bother me," replied Janie. "I still have cleaning to do and you'll make me burn that roast in the oven. You know I like to have everything perfect when people come over, especially tonight." Pausing for a second, she grabbed one edge of the homemade apron she wore and wiped a tear from her eye. "Doesn't she remind you of our own dear Edna? She would have been about Sheila's age had she … lived."

Sensing that his good intentions had failed, Ron slowly raised himself up and walked across to where Janie stood. Putting his arms around her, he inhaled the scent of the lavender perfume he had given her on her birthday and thanked God for the forty years of love they had shared.

"Yes, my dear, t…t-that w…w-would be about right. I'm glad t…t-that w…w-we both like her. Maybe t…t-this w…w-will be t…t-the start of many visits. I w…w-wonder w…w-who she is bringing w…w-with her?"

Just then, the doorbell rang, right on time. Ron opened the door and saw Sheila standing there, holding a bag. She was not alone - there was a tall handsome young man standing by her side.

"W…w-welcome t…t-to our home. Come on in and get out of t…t-this bad w…, rain."

"Thank you. Ron, this is my … friend, Jerry."

"W…w-well, hi t…t-there, Jerry. Glad t..t-to meet you."

"Thanks. I hope that I'm not intruding. Sheila told me how much she liked you and, well, I wanted to meet you."

"No problem at all. Any friend of Sheila's is a friend of mine." Feeling the light touch of a hand on his shoulder, Ron quickly added, "T…t-this is my w…w-wife, Janie."

Janie stood next to him, beaming with pride. "Hello … Ron, make yourself useful - take their coats." The living room was comfortably furnished with overstuffed furniture and a few vintage pieces. Reaching for Sheila's arm, and with Jerry following closely behind, she guided her to the sofa. "Have a seat. Dinner will be ready in a minute. Excuse me, I've got a roast in the oven."

Trying to be as inconspicuous as possible, Sheila put the bag she carried on the floor by her purse. Jerry saw her and curious as to why she didn't give it to Janie asked, "I thought you brought that for them?"

Starting to answer with something that might satisfy his curiosity, Sheila said, "Well, I ..," but was interrupted by Ron as he returned from hanging their coats in the hall closet next to the bedroom.

"I'm so happy you didn't let the w… w-weather stop you from coming t…t-today. Janie has been killing herself for t…t-three days pulling everything t…t-together." Laughing, Ron looked at Sheila and said, "You know how you w…w-women are."

Seeing an opportunity to score some bonus points with Sheila, Jerry said, "Yeah, I guess I've been guilty of that myself." It worked like a charm. Reaching for Jerry's hand and playing with his bracelets was a move that did not go unnoticed by Ron.

"Nothing short of an outright hurricane could have kept us away," said Sheila. "The past few weeks have been terrible for me. I don't know why but I've always been a little afraid of cemeteries. Knowing that you ... and Jerry are around gives me … peace of mind."

"T…t-times like t…t-this are t…t-tough for anyone t…t-to go t…t-through. I've w…w-worked here for many years. I could t…t-tell you some stories about t…t-things t…t-that have happened and w…w-what I've seen people do in this place. One day…"

Just then, Janie walked in. "Now Ron, no one wants to hear those old ghost tales. Sheila, I understand that you are from Houston?"

"Yes, I've lived here all my life. So has Jerry."

"And what do you do?" asked Janie.

"I'm a fashion designer."

"Oh that's wonderful." Turning her attention to Jerry, she was curious about who he was and his relationship with Sheila. Her husband not cold in the grave and she was ...being so familiar with him. Giving Sheila a sheepish look, she raised one hand to her mouth and giggled, "And how did you meet this cutie pie?"

Feeling the warmth of a blush move across his face, Jerry smiled, obviously pleased by the comment. "Well, we ..."

Just then, the scent of meat on the edge of burning floated across the room. "Oh, put a pin in that," said Janie. "My roast is done. Everybody, let's move to the table."

***

Malik watched as the dark grey BMW eased along the gravel road leading to the parking lot. The driver pulled into the space next to him, lowered his window, but never turned to look at Malik. Petey sat in the passenger seat, nervously fingering something he held in his hand.

"Petey ..."

Petey gazed at him with a poker face. "Where are they, little brother?"

Pointing to the small house next to the parking lot, Malik said, "In there."

"Ok, it's starting to get dark, but there's a light at the door so we can watch from here. Let's see what develops. Oh yeah, this is Edward."

The man driving the car turned to face Malik. The steady drumming of rain drops hitting the metal, along with his accent, caused Malik to strain to understand what he was asking. "Was the woman carrying a bag?"

"Yes …"

Chapter 25

Ron and Janie lived in an older home, with the living and dining room areas combined to create one large space. Janie had set the table using their best crystal, china and silverware. The two women walked ahead, side by side, with Ron and Jerry bringing-up the rear.

Ron leaned close to Jerry, his voice raised just above a whisper. "I didn't w...w-want to say anything in front of Janie. She can get so emotional, but Sheila bears a remarkable resemblance t...t-to our daughter, Edna."

"Will she be here tonight?" asked Jerry.

"No ... she ... died several years ago. An auto accident ... on a rainy night just like t...t-this."

"What are you fellas whispering about?" asked Janie. "Ron, you sit right here at the head; Jerry, you're over there; and Sheila is here next to me." Once seated, Janie said, "Ron, say the blessing, please."

"Yes dear. God is great, God is good, t...t-thank you for our food. Let's eat."

Ron licked his lips as the dishes moved around the table. "I w...w-wish w...w-we could eat like t...t-this every night - roast beef, mashed potatoes, creamed corn, mustard greens, fresh-baked bread and sweet potato pie! But on t...t-the money I make, w...w-well, it's enough t...t-that w...w-we can splurge every once in a w...w-while."

"Janie, you can definitely claim bragging rights tonight," said Sheila. "This is a beautiful table. You and Jerry need to compare notes. He's also quite a cook and knows his way around a kitchen."

"Well," said Jerry, between mouthfuls of roast beef and creamed corn, "I cook to survive. But, this food reminds me of the way my mother cooked, with … love and grace."

Janie felt the tears beginning to well-up in her eyes. Looking at Sheila, she said, "I just can't get over how much you look like our daughter, Edna. Ron and I barely finished high school."

Suddenly she glanced up to the ceiling and her lower lip began to quiver. "We never even had enough money to take a honeymoon. Ron started working right after we got married, then Edna was born. We wanted more for her. We started a college fund when she was just a baby, putting a little something away each month. We saved enough over the years to put her through the Art program at the University. We were so proud of her when she got a scholarship in her senior year to study abroad. The accident happened while she was over there in England - driving in bad weather."

Then, turning to Jerry, she said, " … and Jerry, had she lived, you're exactly the kind of man I would have loved to see her marry."

That comment took everyone in the room by surprise. The ting of silverware connecting with china plates was the only sound that filled the next few moments of awkward silence.

Finally Janie said, "Come to think of it Jerry, you never got to tell me how you and Sheila met."

Sensing Jerry's hesitation, Sheila spoke up. "Would you believe that I found him through the Yellow Pages?"

Janie continued eating but gave Sheila a questioning glance. "That's funny… no *really*."

"That's right," said Jerry. She needed … security expertise."

"Is t…t-that t…t-the kind of business you're in?" asked Ron. "W…w-well, happy t…t-to meet a co-w…w-worker. W…w-what company you w…w-with?"

"I have my own business. I'm also going to the University to get my doctorate degree."

"T…t-that's w…w-what I like to hear. A young man w…w-who is determined t…t-to be somebody special in t…t-this w…w-world."

Janie shot Sheila the kind of knowing look that comes from a lifetime of living. Sensing that there was much more than told, she said, "It's good to have someone you can count on when times get rough. I understand that you recently lost your husband?"

"Yes, I …"

Ron remembered how distraught Sheila was when he first saw her in the columbarium. The look on her face told him that she was still emotionally fragile, not ready to have this conversation. "Now Janie, let's t…t-talk about something - pleasant."

Grateful for the rescue, Sheila continued eating. The dinner almost finished, she glanced at her watch, realizing that it was just about time to set the stage for her departure.

"You know," said Sheila, "I love it when the seasons change in Houston. It's humid and rainy now, but soon we'll get a break when the temperature starts to cool-off. Every year I seem to get something like a cold or maybe a seasonal flu. I don't know, maybe it's really bad allergies? It's been that way ever since I was a child. Like right now - is it just me or is it warm in here? And … oh boy, I'm a little dizzy. I hope I'm not coming down with something. I don't want to spoil the evening."

Both Ron and Janie gave her looks of concern. "Oh heavens," said Janie, "We wouldn't want that to happen. Would you … like to lie down for a while?"

"If it's not too … inconvenient. I feel like such a party-pooper."

"Not at all," said Janie. "You've been though a lot and the weather has been just awful. Come on, you can use our bedroom. I'll get a blanket. We'll find something to do … maybe a card game! I'll get you settled then come back in an hour to check on you."

Jerry stood at the bedroom door as Janie made Sheila comfortable on the bed. Raising an eyebrow at her, he said, "This is rather… sudden isn't it?"

Feigning innocence, Sheila avoided his unwavering stare. "Yes, but maybe it will go away if I get a few minutes rest. I'll be ok."

"Come on Jerry," said Janie. "Let her rest. We'll be in the next room. Ron, get the cards. How about a game of Go Fish?"

"You'll have to teach that one to me," said Jerry, as he closed the bedroom door and went back into the living room. He never noticed that the bag Sheila carried was placed discretely beside the bed.

As soon as the door closed, Sheila sat-up on the bed and looked around the room. It was well-furnished with a full-sized bed covered by a homemade bedspread, chest of drawers, two nightstands with matching paisley table lamps, and a vanity-type dressing table with chair. There was also a small window, probably just big enough for her to squeeze through. And there was something on the dresser that caught her attention - a flashlight and a set of what looked like … keys! Those were Ron's master keys, probably to every door in the chapel and most importantly, to the main door of the columbarium.

Now, if only she could get to her coat. The hallway was dark and the closet was just a few feet from the bedroom door. Quickly getting up from the bed, she walked to the door and cracked it open just wide enough to see that their backs were turned to her. Reaching over to the closet, she lifted Jerry's umbrella and her coat off the rack. Both were still damp from when they arrived. She put her coat on and stuffed Ron's keys into one of the pockets. Picking-up the bag, she opened the window, slipped through and fell to the ground. If she hurried, she could do what she had to do, be back before bed check, and make a miraculous recovery.

Chapter 26

The three men watched the small house from the parking lot, looking for any new development that would break the monotony made worse by the dreary weather. The tension in the air was so thick that it could be cut with a knife. Malik's voice was the first to break the silence. Unable to control his outburst, he yelled, "Hey, someone is coming out of that window."

Edward shot him a dirty look.

"Keep your voice down," he whispered. "You're screaming loud enough to wake the dead!"

Lowering his voice to just above a whisper, Malik said, "Sorry... it looks like ... Sheila?"

"Ok, let's follow her," said Petey. "And Malik, *please* try to be quiet!"

Sheila walked down the stone-path as quickly as she could, trying to avoid stepping into the puddles of water which seemed to be everywhere. It was still light enough for her to see how it wove in-between rows of headstones, some decorated with relics long-sense faded. The day's rain intensified the already foul odor of floral arrangements lingering in the air, once alive but now in various stages of wilt and decay. Finally arriving at the end of the path she saw the columbarium, dark and for-boding in the waning light.

Standing by the door, she reached into her coat pocket and pulled-out Ron's keys. Finding the one fitting the lock, she pushed the door open and walked into the lobby. The building was not alarmed, probably because the cemetery was small and not on a main street. Turning-on the flashlight, she walked through the corridors until coming to Thomas' niche.

Petey, Malik and Edward were hot on her trail. Reaching the door, Petey pulled Malik aside.

"Malik, remember when we talked about … Plan B, uh, pushing-up daisies?"

Malik looked at him like he was speaking a foreign language. "You started but didn't finish. What's Plan B?"

"Well, it's obvious that Sheila has a new man in her life. That rules-out any possibility for the two of you getting together. See where I'm going? If what's in that bag is what I think it is…then, I'm sorry, she's got to … die."

"Yeah," said Edward, "and I'm holding just what's needed to get the job done. We can even dump the body right here in this cemetery. There must be a fresh grave that we can use around here, somewhere."

"What are you talking about?" Malik said, "You promised me …"

Not only did Edward enjoy the blowup between the brothers, he looked for a way to keep it going. Trying his best to sound sympathetic, he said, "Since it's dark and there's no-one in here but us … well, I don't see why the boy can't have a few minutes of … fun with her, before we…" *If only her husband was here to see that!*

"Maybe..." said Petey. "Yeah, that might be fun to ... watch."

Malik stood there, his hooded eyes wide, glaring at his big brother. His own brother, the one that he wanted to please most in this life, was going to deprive him of his trophy? He didn't want Sheila dead, he wanted to ... keep her around, control her, use her, make her his whether she liked it or not.

"That's not what I want," he said. "I need ... time to work her. Just let me get my hands on her. I know how to break her down. She's not that much of a threat."

"Oh, yes she is," said Petey. "She took something from Edwards' office that could get us- him and me, in a world of trouble. Grow-up, little brother. You can't always have what you want the way you want it in this life. Count your blessings. Take what you can get. And, be satisfied with what you can buy with that money. Edward, give me the gun."

Walking into the building, Malik lunged at Petey, trying to get the gun away from him.

"We don't have time for this. You crazy mother ... let go, Malik, *let go!*"

Hearing the sound of gunfire, Sheila turned off the flashlight. She could see the outline of figures standing in the doorway, struggling and cursing. But, she wasn't the only one who heard the ruckus. Even though the card game was still going on at the house, Ron heard the noise and was the first to react. He ran into the bedroom closely followed by Jerry and Janie.

Jerry was livid as he stared at the empty bed. "So that's what she had in that bag. I told her not to do it. I warned her. *She promised me!*"

"W…w-what are you t…t-talking about?" said Ron, trying his best to make sense of what Jerry said.

"It's a long story. Right now, I need you to tell me - where is the columbarium?"

Ron stared at Jerry, his face ashen and visibly shaken. *Was that where she went? Why, in God's name would she go there?*

With a shrug of resignation, Ron said, "I'll t…t-take you t…t-there. Janie, stay in t…t-the house and call t…t-the police."

"Ron …"

"Just do it, honey. And, stay here!"

Jerry sprinted across the hallowed ground to the columbarium. Trying his best to keep-up, Ron arrived just in time to see him staring at a body lying prone in the doorway. It was Malik's body, blood mixing with the rain, running in streams down the stone path.

Frantic to be heard, Ron yelled, "Jerry don't go in t…t-there. You don't have a w…w-weapon. W…w-wait for the cops."

As if he had suddenly gone deaf, Jerry ignored his plea. He yelled, "Sheila, where are you?"

A frightened voice answered from somewhere in the darkness, "Here … I'm here Jerry."

Stepping over Malik's body, Jerry charged into the lobby, trying to follow the sound of her voice, not knowing that two men, armed and dangerous, watched and waited.

Chapter 27

The detectives looked at each other. This time, Detective Riley spoke first. "Mrs. Palmer, you heard Petey yelling that he shot his little brother, Malik?"

"Yes. I recognized his voice. I also heard Edward talking, but I couldn't make-out everything he said. Then, Jerry called-out to me and I answered him, trying not to let Petey and Edward know where I was."

***

Edward and Petey cowered behind a bench in one of the corridors not far from Sheila. "Man keep it together. We got to think quickly," said Edward. "You still got the gun?"

Petey felt like he was unable to wake-up from his own worst nightmare. Heart pounding and waves of nausea surging through his stomach, he wailed "Malik … I just shot my little brother… Malik. I didn't mean to do it. He jumped at me - the gun went off…"

"Yeah, well …" said Edward curtly. "Now we got to think about ourselves. Where's that bitch?"

"I think she's over there," said Petey, his finger shaking as he pointed in the direction of one of the dark corridors. Unfortunately it was the one where Sheila was hiding.

"Ok, you go around that way and we'll trap her in between us. It's dark in here and … maybe we can finish our business and get out before the cops come. Petey - *get that bag!*"

There was no escape route for Sheila. Boxed-in as she was, her best hope was that Jerry would find her first. She turned-on the flashlight, hoping to let just enough of the beam shine for him to discover her.

Sheila heard the shuffle of feet coming toward her. Thinking that it was Jerry, she whispered, "I'm over here."

"Yeah, bitch, we see you!"

In the gleam of the flashlight, she saw the faces of two men, their mouths twisted into horrible grimaces, their eyes blazing with satisfaction.

"Where's the bag?" said Edward. "Give it up… and *maybe* we'll let you live."

Hoping that they wouldn't notice what she was doing, Sheila eased the bag under the bench with her foot. "I don't know what you're talking about. Get out of my way."

It was Edward who made the discovery. "There it is. Well, if that's the way you want it… Petey, give me the gun so I can shoot her and we can get out of here."

"Don't even try it." It was Jerry's voice, powerful, authoritative, ringing-out loud and clear.

"So, *you're* the mystery man," said Edward. "Well, say goodbye."

Sheila screamed. The shot fired hit its target. Jerry fell to the floor grasping his chest, the blood starting to stain his already rain-soaked shirt.

Chapter 28

Against his better judgement, Ron followed Jerry into the lobby. Never having been in the building after dark, he wasn't quite sure where the light switch was located. Running his hands along the wall, he finally found it and pushed the on button. The stormy weather had caused a power outage, but the emergency lights were still working. Eerie as the red glow was, Ron was thankful for the added visibility. Cautiously making his way across the building, he rounded the end of the corridor which put him directly behind Petey and Edward. Then he saw Sheila, the anguish on her face evident as she knelt beside Jerry, still conscious enough to know what was going on around him but growing weaker by the moment.

Knowing that the cops were on their way, his first impulse was to retrace his footsteps. But, try as he might, Ron was unable to move from where he stood. Instead, he felt beads of sweat popping-up on his forehead. *Did the power outage trip the heater by accident?* Ron could feel his shoulders pulling backward as his body became more erect. He was going into a trance, but this time it was lighter, so he was aware of everything going on around him. He started walking toward the men who weren't aware of his presence until he was almost standing directly behind them. Just as they turned to face him, something happened that drew the attention of everyone present.

A white light, punctuated by flashes of blue light, flowed from the niche containing Thomas' ashes. Dim at first, it grew brighter until it was almost blinding. The energy in the room shifted causing Sheila to feel tingling sensations run up and down her arms with a massaging motion that was strangely pleasant.

Edward and Petey stood still as statues, eyes wide and filled with terror, gazing with a kind of fascinated horror at the image materializing before them. Thomas stood there in the light, looking as he did the first time Sheila saw him at the gym. Passing between them, the specter hovered in front of Petey. Momentarily confused, Edward fired at it not realizing that he was actually hitting Petey.

His mouth open and unable to speak, Edward stared in disbelief at Petey's lifeless body on the floor.

Feeling more like a spectator in a movie theatre, Sheila heard a familiar voice coming from Ron's lips, words flowing clear and without interruption. Then she realized everything was happening in real-time. Sadness clouded the face of the specter as he gazed at her. Suddenly she felt no fear, only sorrow and a longing for something that could never be satisfied.

"Sheila, I had no idea that being in Spirit would have certain - advantages. Confused thinking becomes crystal clear. Now I'm going to tell you what you must hear. Life is a journey. As individuals, we each choose different paths to follow. Some have more challenges than others, but the goal is the same - to make decisions that let us thrive, evolve, and prepare for the transition every human eventually faces.

There are events, often beyond our control, which need to happen before others so that the journey can be successful. We see them as unfair, but in reality they are only roadblocks that get in the way. The challenge is to remove them so the journey can continue. The world is full of people who come into each other's lives for just this purpose. I came into your life to help you clear a roadblock so you could move on and eventually be with someone very ... special.

I always had feelings for you, but because of our age difference, letting you know was a matter of timing. Years ago when visiting my friends, I passed your house and watched you as a young girl playing in your front yard - hazel eyes, curly brown hair and creamy tanned skin - a little angel innocent and untouched by the cruelty of life. Working-out at the gym, I watched you mature into a woman, longing to express your femininity but fearing that others would think you weak, vulnerable and unworthy of their respect.

Life can play cruel tricks. I was just a regular guy, decent and law abiding. That was my *true self*, but I didn't think I was good enough for you as I was. You were starting your journey and wouldn't notice or respect that kind of man, especially one who was low on cash. What was it they called you? Oh yes, *Miss Thing* - "with champagne wishes and caviar dreams."

Back then you wanted material things and to go places where only big bucks could take you. You were an *impossible* dream, but I wanted you and was willing to do whatever it took to make you want me, even if it meant loosing my most precious possession - my *true self*, in the process. So, I had a decision to make. I could have offered you a love based on honesty, loyalty, and

146

unselfishness, but my fear of rejection was so great that it kept me from even trying. That was my challenge - the roadblock that I had to overcome and I failed miserably.

Instead, I began creating my mask - one that would hide my *true self.* I would become a "winner" - a man who could get the big bucks to show you how attractive being with me could be - a man of the world with status, cars, clothes, and the ability to give you - security. Secretly, I longed for the day when I could take off that mask, reveal my *true self* to you, but only after I was sure that you wouldn't leave me. You weren't the only one afraid of ... rejection.

I didn't realize that wearing a mask is like being in a self-imposed prison. You see, all masks are deceptions by definition and what a tangled web I wove.

I became comfortable wearing my mask. I made poor choices in associates and poorer ones in activities. The money flowed in, but it was dirty. I got in over my head and my past mistakes caught up with me. In my greed I became selfish and dismissed any thought of where my actions might eventually take me.

The irony was how I eventually compromised the relationship and misused the person that I valued the most in life. I tried to control you, turn you into someone I could use for my own purposes - your bank accounts, your good name, because after all, you would reap the benefits. But please understand that it took two to tango. The mask you wore was that of a woman who tolerated that treatment, even found ways to justify it and not rock the boat. Misery loves company. I had some satisfaction knowing that both of us, in our own ways, had taken the low road.

Then you did something that I ... wouldn't, something that changed everything for both of us. Not satisfied with our relationship, you stayed with me, unselfishly helped me and gave me the best that you had with no strings attached. That was the *caring* part of you, your *true self*, that you tried to hide. The moment you felt the joy that came from letting *your* light shine was the necessary event that changed the course of your journey. That was when you broke free from your self-imposed prison. You took the high road. You removed your mask to reveal the woman you were all along. The way was clear for you to continue your journey.

I saw how it transformed you for the better, and the joy it brought into your life. It was then that you understood what *true love* meant. I envied you for your courage and resolve. Was it possible for me to get a second chance? Perhaps there was something left in me of the decent and honest man I once was. If I could only take off my mask, I *would* free him from his prison. Then the scales of life would be balanced. What you had become was a woman who could respect that kind of man - the kind of man she truly deserved. Unfortunately, fate stepped in before I could make it happen."

There were no words for what she felt. But, somehow Sheila suspected that the specter, Thomas, understood what was truly in her heart. Looking at the specter through tears running down her cheeks, Sheila said, "Thomas, I'm truly sorry for how things turned out."

With the sudden brightening of his face, Sheila knew that her suspicion was accurate. "Sheila, we reap what we sow and there are consequences for choices. You are a good person. You became your own woman and that set you free from what I had planned for you. I wronged you and I am deeply sorry for that. Now I can make it up to you. I know everything that's happened since I transitioned - about how you wanted to clear my name and about ... you and Jerry, what he gives you that I can't. Now I know what it means to give and receive ... *higher love.* You and Jerry taught me that. Everything that I was that ran counter to that has been ... released. Only the good remains."

" But, you're ... dead," moaned Sheila. "Isn't it too late to ... change?"

"Not at all. There is no ... death, just transition. I no longer have a physical body, but my ... energy continues. You must understand. What you went through with me was necessary. You wanted to uncover the truth, so you contacted the person best qualified to help you - a private detective. Choosing Jerry was not by accident. Didn't you wonder why it was so easy to connect with him at a deeper level, or why you felt like you had known him forever? It's because, he is your *true twin flame!* Now he is ... transitioning. He might have a chance to ... continue with you, if I give my energy to him. After that's done, the doctors can treat his physical body. He is the better man - the one who you can give and receive *true love* from, unconditionally. What I will do, I do freely. He will stay with you and live a full life... and, in a way I'll get a second chance. My *true self,* the honest and decent part, will also be with you. In that way, *our* team will endure. You'll have the best of both of us. It's up to you."

Sheila looked at the man she held in her arms, remembering their time together and contemplating the possibilities that the future might hold. Jerry, aware of all that had been said, gave his consent with a smile that was barely perceptible.

With tears of gratitude welling up in her eyes, Sheila pleaded, "Yes Thomas, do it, *do it*." With that, the blue light faded taking the image of Thomas with it. Glass shattered, the urn crashed to the floor, and ashes gently floated in the air like black snowflakes. The sweet spicy scent of chocolate filled the corridor as Jerry opened his eyes, now sea-foam green with just a *hint* of black, smiled at her and said, "What's up .. *dark and stormy*?"

Chapter 29

Both detectives could tell that Sheila was leaving out some of the details of what happened in that corridor by the niche. "So Petey killed Malik, Edward killed Petey and also wounded Jerry. That accounts for all of the bodies," said Detective Patterson. "But, what would make him kill Petey?"

Pursing her lips together, Sheila said, "I wonder about that too. Must have gotten spooked or something. It was dark in there and you know how scary being in a place like that can be."

"And what about the bag?" asked Detective Riley.

"Everything happened so fast. I was going to put it in the niche but didn't have time. You'll find it under the bench. There's a file in there with enough evidence to convict Edward of Thomas' murder and put him away for a very long time."

"Ok. Our team is still in there. The whole place is a crime scene. I'll radio them to get it."

"Yeah ... losing his license is just the start," smirked Detective Riley. "We'll get him on Murder One, medical malpractice ... hell, he'll die in the joint. We'll even go after the hospital for coverup of medical malpractice. Heads are going to roll before this is over."

"And, there's one other thing," said Sheila. "I think you'll find something in that file about ... oversea bank accounts."

Detective Patterson's whole face lit-up in sheer joy. Momentarily forgetting all about his lumbago, he jumped-up from his chair and sounding just like Clint Eastwood said, "Make my day!"

"Oh, by the way, what happened to Edward and Ron?" asked Sheila.

Embarrassed by his outburst, Detective Patterson tried his best to assume a professional posture. But, he couldn't stifle his laughter in response to Sheila's question. "We found Ron, standing at the end of the corridor, looking like he was coming down from some kind of bad drug trip. He was alert enough to give us a statement; so, your story was verified. He's ok, resting peacefully at home with his wife, Janie."

Then his expression hardened as he said, "Now Edward, that's another story. We got there just in time to see him running out of the columbarium, screaming like a banshee some kind of nonsense about seeing a ghost." Looking at Sheila with his eyebrows raised and a half-smile on his face, he said, "Nonsense, that's all it really was, *wasn't* it Mrs. Palmer?"

"Of course, detective, of course."

"Anyway," he added, "he still had the gun in his hand. And by the way, the guy's from forensics called. Edward and Petey's fingerprints were all over it, not yours. Mrs. Palmer, you're free to go."

"What about my going into Edwards office?"

"Under the circumstances," said Detective Patterson, "I'm going to recommend to the district attorney that the charges be dropped. Technically breaking and entering is a criminal act and you would have to come before a judge. You bent the law to make sure the bad guy would be caught. If you didn't get jail time, there would at least be some kind of probation period, maybe community service. But, you have been more than cooperative. I'm, sure my *partner* will support that recommendation."

He called me his partner. Smiling, Detective Riley replied, "Yes, my *partner* speaks for both of us."

Once again, the hollow sound of knuckles rapping at the door could be heard. Detective Patterson rose slowly from his chair. This time he was very aware of the discomfort caused by his lumbago as he walked across the room. He held a brief conversation with another detective in the hallway, then returned to the table where Sheila and his partner sat.

With a twinkle in his blue eyes, he said, "Besides, I'm sure you're going to have your hands full helping Jerry recuperate from his injuries. The hospital called - he's out of danger. In fact, his wounds are healing *much* faster than expected. They're still trying to figure-out why. Off the record, you and Jerry really had a thing going on, didn't you? It's not a crime-maybe questionable judgement, but not a crime."

Sheila smiled. "Why, Detective Patterson. Is that your nose I see twitching?"

***

Detectives Patterson and Riley left the building, heading to their respective homes to catch a few hours rest and relaxation before returning to start another day. They walked side by side as equals, processing all that had happened. Edward was just small fry. Those oversea bank accounts - that was big time stuff! Yes, Sheila's method was unorthodox, but thanks to her, the pay-off was more than imagined.

"I think we work well as a team, don't you?" said Detective Patterson. "That was a tough case and I like the way you handled yourself. There's a lot we can teach and learn from each other. Having you tied down with so much paperwork is a waste of your talent. That's going to change, and soon. You know, our kind of work can be challenging and it's good to have someone to chew the fat with. Oh yeah, a group of us get together every Friday - go out, have some beer and burgers, just unwind. Can you make it?"

Sensing the sincerity in his invitation, Detective Riley replied, "Yes, I'd love to." Laughing she added, "You go on ahead. I forgot something."

"Ok, partner, see you in a few hours."

Once inside the building, Detective Riley went straight to her cubicle. Opening the top desk drawer where she kept her secret notebook, her *little treasures*, she tore the pages out, one by one, then fed them into the paper shredder on her desk.

***

"Ron," said Janie. "I wonder whatever happened to that nice couple, Sheila and Jerry? I hope they come back to visit one day. By the way, this letter came in the mail today. There's no return address, so I wonder who might have sent it."

"It's addressed t…t-to us, all right. Let's see …" said Ron. Carefully tearing-open one side, he shook the envelop causing the contents to fall on the table. "Janie, t…t-there are t…t-ten one-hundred dollar bills in here plus t…t-two, round t…t-trip t…t-tickets t…t-to Jamaica, and reservations for t…t-two w…w-weeks at some place called Sandals Resort in Montego Bay. W...w-wait a minute! Here's a note. It says t...t-the "Honeymoon Suite" has been reserved in our names. Can you beat t...t-that!"

Adah F. Kennon

About the Author

Born in Houston, Texas, Dr. Adah F. Kennon also lived in northern California and Maryland prior to settling in Las Vegas, Nevada with her husband (now deceased). She worked for 31 years as a School Psychologist in two states, holds five advanced degrees in the areas of psychology, education and counseling (BA, 3 Master's Degrees, Ph.D.), and is a Certified Clinical Mental Health Counselor (retired). She entered the entertainment industry in 2012, started her own business (Sheba Enterprises), broadened her acting and voice-over acting performance skills, and was the host/producer of a weekly hour-long radio talk show (Possibilities with Dr. Adah Kennon). She has been recognized in ICE Magazine (*Inner Circle Executive Magazine for High Achieving Business Professionals, Continental Who's Who*) as a "Pinnacle Professional, Top Professional Woman." She has also been featured in Top 100 Industry Experts in America Magazine (*National Association of Distinguished Professionals, Covington Who's Who*). A published author, Dr. Kennon has competed in body-building competitions, appeared as a run-way model for local charity events, and been featured in a body-building magazine. She is an environmentalist, social activist, and enjoys gardening and traveling.

Visit her websites at
 www.247lightheartedcaregivers.com
and www.adahkennonauthor.com.

Made in USA - Kendallville, IN
1213204_9780578813912
12.15.2020 0824